Poached

"Oh, there you are, Nancy," Hannah said, wiping her hands on her apron. "You just missed a phone call. The young lady sounded rather upset! Her number is on the pad."

"Thanks." I hurried to look at the notepad next to the phone. Simone's name and phone number were written there in Hannah's neat cursive. "Oh! That's the new owner of the Peterson place. We met her this afternoon. I wonder what she wants?"

Figuring there was only one way to find out, I dialed the number. Simone answered, though she sounded so upset that I almost didn't recognize her voice. "Nancy!" she cried when I identified myself. "I am so glad to hear from you. As you know, Pierre and I have met almost no one here in River Heights yet, and I didn't know where else to turn."

"What is it, Simone?" I asked anxiously. The worried crackle in her voice told me that something was wrong—very wrong.

"It's my Fabergé egg," Simone replied. "I walked into the living room and noticed that it's gone!"

Look out for other books about

NANCY DREW
Girl Detective

#1 Without a Trace
#2 A Race Against Time

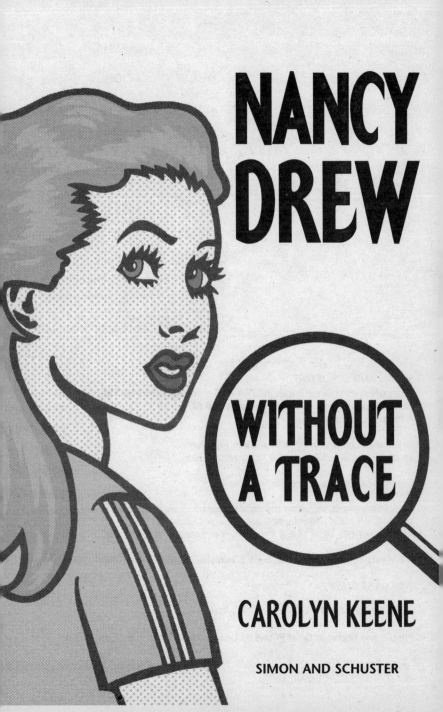

NANCY DREW

WITHOUT A TRACE

CAROLYN KEENE

SIMON AND SCHUSTER

SIMON AND SCHUSTER
First published in Great Britain in 2004 by Simon & Schuster UK Ltd.
Africa House, 64-78 Kingsway, London WC2B 6AH
A Viacom Company.

Originally published in 2004 by Aladdin Paperbacks,
an imprint of Simon & Schuster Children's Division, New York.

A CIP catalogue record for this book is available from the British Library upon request.

ISBN 0 689 87498 7

1 3 5 7 9 10 8 6 4 2

Printed and bound in Great Britain by Cox & Wyman Ltd.

CONTENTS

1	*Friends and Neighbours*	1
2	*Party Plans*	18
3	*A Call for Help*	25
4	*A Stolen Heirloom*	36
5	*Leads and Clues*	48
6	*Messy Motives*	55
7	*Gathering Clues*	66
8	*The Shadowy Figure*	80
9	*Stalking the Truth*	89
10	*Connections and Opportunities*	109
11	*Accidents and Answers*	123
12	*A Taste of Friendship*	134

Friends and Neighbors

My name is Nancy Drew. My friends tell me I'm always looking for trouble, but that's not really true. It just seems to have a way of finding me.

Take last week, for instance. I arrived home on Friday afternoon from a volunteer luncheon and stepped into the house to hear the sound of shouting.

". . . and if something isn't done about this, things are going to get ugly!" The angry voice rang through the empty front hallway. "I can guarantee that!"

"Uh-oh," I muttered, immediately on the alert. I didn't recognize the voice, but I have a sort of sixth sense about anything odd or mysterious, and it started tingling right away. The shouting man sounded intense. Desperate, even. Definitely not business as usual for a quiet, lazy, Midwestern summer day.

I hurried toward the source of the voice: my father's office. Dad has been both father and mother to me ever since my mom died when I was three years old, and I happen to think he's pretty great. And I'm not the only one who thinks so. If you ask anyone in our hometown of River Heights to name the best, most honest and respected attorney in town, Carson Drew will always be at the top of their list. His main office is downtown, but he also sometimes sees clients in the cozy, wood-paneled office on the first floor of our spacious colonial house.

Tiptoeing toward the office, I brushed my shoulder-length hair out of the way and carefully pressed my ear to the door's polished oak surface. My friends would probably call it eavesdropping. I prefer to call it staying informed.

My father was speaking now. "Let's just settle down for a moment," he said in his calmest, most authoritative voice. "I'm sure we can get to the bottom of this."

"I certainly hope so!" the other man exclaimed, though his voice was a little quieter now. "If not, I'm perfectly ready to press charges. This is a violation of my rights as a tax-paying property owner."

I tried to place the voice, which was beginning to seem familiar. It took me a second to notice the sound of footsteps walking toward the door. I jumped back

2

just in time to avoid falling on my face as the door swung open into the office.

"Nancy!" My father raised an eyebrow in my direction as he exited his office, obviously a little displeased to find me lurking in the hallway. A portly, well-dressed man walked out after him, his wavy gray hair in a mess, and beads of sweat dotting his brow. Dad gestured toward him. "You know our neighbor, Bradley Geffington."

"Oh, right!" I exclaimed as the familiar voice clicked into place in my mind. Not only does Bradley Geffington live a couple of blocks away, but he manages the local bank where Dad and I have our accounts. "Er, that is, of course I know him. Nice to see you, Mr. Geffington."

"Hello, Nancy." Bradley Geffington shook my hand, though he still seemed distracted and a little annoyed. He glanced over at my father. "I'm not going to rest until I get to the bottom of this, Carson," he said. "If Harold Safer is behind the damage to my property, he's going to pay. Mark my words."

I blinked in surprise. Harold Safer is another homeowner in our quiet, tree-lined riverside neighborhood. He also owns the local cheese shop. He's a little eccentric, but generally mild mannered and well liked.

"Excuse me, Mr. Geffington," I said. "If you don't

3

mind my asking, just what is it that Mr. Safer has done to you?"

Bradley Geffington shrugged. "I don't mind at all," he said. "I want everyone to know, so no one else will have to go through this. He demolished my zucchini!"

"Your zucchini?" I repeated. It wasn't quite what I was expecting to hear. "Um, what do you mean?"

"Yes, why don't you give Nancy all the details?" Dad spoke up. "She's the amateur detective in the family. Maybe she can help you get to the bottom of things. Then we can figure out how to proceed from there."

Dad sounded slightly bemused. I guess you'd have to know Dad as well as I do to have picked up on it. He always takes his cases very seriously—he knows his clients count on him to help them in their darkest hours. But after all his famous trials, huge lawsuits, and important summaries in front of grand juries, I'm sure he never expected anyone to ask him to initiate a suit over *zucchini*!

Luckily Bradley Geffington didn't seem to notice a thing. "Yes, I've heard that Nancy has a certain talent for solving mysteries." He gazed at me thoughtfully. "Very well, then. Here are the facts. I had a thriving zucchini patch going in my garden as of Tuesday afternoon. Five plants. At least half a dozen beautiful, perfect zucchinis almost ready to pick. I could almost

4

taste them grilled and sautéed and baked into zucchini bread...." He clasped his hands together, smacked his lips, and then shook his head sadly.

"What happened?" I asked.

"I woke up Wednesday morning and headed outside to water the garden before work as usual. That's when I found them—my zucchini. Or at least, what was left of them." His voice shook slightly and he closed his eyes, clearly upset at the memory. "It looked as if someone had taken a club to them. Little green bits and pieces everywhere!"

"That's terrible." It did sound like vandalism of some sort, although I couldn't imagine why anyone would bother to vandalize a bunch of zucchini. "But what makes you think it was Mr. Safer who did it?"

Bradley Geffington rolled his eyes. "He's been moaning and complaining all summer about how my tomato cages block the view of his blasted sunsets."

I hid a smile. Aside from selling an amazing variety of cheese in his shop, Harold Safer is well known around town for two things: his twin obsessions for Broadway theater and sunsets. He travels east to New York City a couple of times every year and spends a week or two seeing every Broadway show he possibly can. And he built a huge deck on the back of his house, overlooking the river, for the express purpose of watching the sun set over the bluffs each and every evening.

However, Harold Safer is also well known for being kind and sensitive. He even rescues stranded worms from the sidewalk in front of his house after it rains. I couldn't imagine him taking a club to anything, let alone someone else's garden.

"Okay," I said tactfully. "But if it was your tomatoes that are troubling him, why would he attack your zucchini?"

"Don't ask me!" Bradley Geffington exclaimed. "You're the detective—you figure it out. All I know is that my whole zucchini crop is ruined, and he's the only one who could have done it." He glanced at his watch. "I've got to go. My lunch break is almost over, and I want to stop by the garden center and see if they still have any zucchini plants."

Dad and I walked him to the front door. As Dad closed the door behind our neighbor, he glanced at me. "Do you mind looking into this?" he asked. "I know it's a bit silly, but I hate to think of something like this coming between two good neighbors."

I nodded, realizing he was right. Besides, if there really was someone wandering around the neighborhood smashing things with a mallet, it was probably best to find out who and why.

"I'll do what I can," I promised. "Bess and George

6

are supposed to come by any minute now. We were supposed to go shopping, but I'm sure they'll be willing to help out with a little sleuthing instead."

As if on cue, the doorbell rang. I hurried to open it and found my two best friends standing there.

Even though they're cousins, it never ceases to amaze me how different Bess Marvin and George Fayne are from each other. If you looked up the word *girl* in the dictionary, you'd find Bess's picture there to illustrate it. She's pretty, blond, and curvy in all the right places, with dimples in both cheeks and a wardrobe full of flowery dresses and lots of delicate jewelry that sets off her perfect features. But angular, athletic-looking George prefers jeans to jewelry. She keeps her dark hair cut short and is quick to correct anyone who calls her by her given name, Georgia.

Dad greeted my friends, then returned to his office. As I led Bess and George into the living room, I quickly filled them in on the zucchini smasher.

"You're kidding, right?" George commented in her usual blunt way. "Are you really so desperate for a mystery that you're going to investigate *this*?"

Bess giggled. "Be nice, George," she chided. "Poor Nancy hasn't had a burglar to bust or a kidnapper to capture in . . . what? At least a couple of weeks? Who can blame her for being desperate?"

"I know, I know," I said with a smile. "It's not much

of a case. But I want to figure out what's really going on before it causes trouble between Mr. Geffington and Mr. Safer. It would be terrible if they actually went to court over something so foolish. This could ruin their friendship forever."

"That's true," Bess agreed.

"Good," I said. "Does that mean you're going to help me?"

Bess looked a little disappointed; she loves shopping. But then she smiled gamely. "I suppose so," she said.

George nodded. "Besides," she added with a sly grin. "Maybe investigating the Case of the Vegetable Vandal will help keep Nancy away from any *real* trouble!"

A few minutes later the three of us found ourselves seated in the comfortably elegant living room of Mrs. Cornelius Mahoney, who lives down the street from Bradley Geffington. Two other neighbors, Ms. Thompson and Mrs. Zucker, were there as well. As soon as we'd arrived on her doorstep, Mrs. Mahoney had graciously insisted that we come in out of the hot sun and join them for tea.

"There you go, girls," Mrs. Mahoney said in her thin, reedy voice, her kind hazel eyes twinkling beneath her neat gray bangs as she set a tray of drinks in front of us. "Some ice tea for a warm day. And please do help yourselves to the cookies." She gestured to a huge platter of baked goodies on the polished mahogany coffee table.

"Now *this* is what I call investigating," George whispered to me as she leaned forward to help herself to several cookies. No matter how many sweets George eats, her slim frame never gains an ounce—a fact that is a constant source of irritation to her curvy cousin.

Ellen Zucker, thirtysomething and attractive, smiled at me and stirred her tea. "So Nancy, how are your father and Hannah? Please tell Hannah I really enjoyed her recipe for . . . excuse me a moment." Mrs. Zucker stood and hurried toward the open front window. "Owen!" she called out. "I told you, if you're going to play out there by yourself you need to stay away from the street. Why don't you play in the backyard for a while instead?"

My friends and I exchanged an amused glance. Energetic four-year-old Owen Zucker had been playing baseball in the driveway when we'd arrived. All of us had taken our turns baby-sitting him in the past, and we all knew it only took a moment to lose track of the active, energetic little boy.

Mrs. Zucker sighed and sat down again. "Poor Owen," she said. "I'm afraid he must get terribly bored following me around from house to house like

9

this. I've been out visiting throughout the neighborhood all week raising money for the Anvil Day fireworks display."

I smiled, knowing that Mrs. Zucker had come to the right house for that. Mrs. Mahoney is one of the wealthiest people in town. Her late husband was the only descendant of Ethan Mahoney, who founded the Mahoney Anvil Corporation back in the early nineteenth century. The anvil business is long gone, except for the town's annual Anvil Day celebration, but the Mahoney fortune is bigger than ever. When Cornelius was alive, most of that fortune went toward classic cars and obscure financial schemes. According to all sources, old Cornelius was a stingy, mean-spirited man who never revealed a kind or likable side in public. But Mrs. Mahoney is a generous soul who is beloved by all who meet her. Her bountiful contributions to various charities have gone a long way toward repairing the reputation of the Mahoney name.

"I imagine Owen knows how to entertain himself," Bess commented, glancing out the window as the little boy scurried around the corner of the house, ball and bat in hand. "I remember the last time I baby-sat him—he decided he wanted to make cookies, and had everything in the refrigerator out on the floor before I could get across the kitchen to stop him."

"That sounds like my Owen!" Mrs. Zucker exclaimed as the other women laughed.

"Now then, what brings you girls here today?" Ms. Thompson asked. She is a bright, birdlike woman in her forties who is on a couple of volunteer committees with me. She works as a nurse at the local hospital. "Are you on the trail of another exciting mystery, Nancy?"

I smiled sheepishly as my friends chuckled. Did I mention that I'm sort of famous around town for solving mysteries?

"Well, sort of," I admitted. "It seems that someone has been causing trouble in Mr. Geffington's vegetable patch."

Mrs. Zucker gasped. "Really?" she exclaimed. "The same thing happened at my house! Someone stomped all over my zucchini a couple of nights ago."

Very interesting. Mrs. Zucker lives across the street and a few houses down from Mr. Geffington.

"Do you have any idea who might have done it?" I asked.

Mrs. Zucker shook her head. "I figured it was just some teenagers on a dare, or maybe animals," she said. "It must have happened while I was out collecting for Anvil Day after dinner that night. I was out quite late, my husband was downtown at a business dinner, and Owen was probably playing a game with a sitter I hired for the night, so none of us would have noticed a thing. I didn't really think much about it beyond that, especially since neither my husband nor Owen likes zucchini much anyway."

"I don't blame them," George said, reaching for another cookie. "I hate the stuff myself."

"So you didn't see the culprit," I mused. I looked at the other two women. "What about you? Did either of you notice anything strange going on in the neighborhood three nights ago?"

"Not me," Mrs. Mahoney said. "Have you asked any of the other neighbors? Harold Safer lives on that side of Bluff Street. Maybe he saw something."

Her comment reminded me of something. "I heard that the old Peterson place just sold," I said, referring to Mr. Geffington's other next-door neighbor. "Do any of you know who bought it?"

"I do," Ms. Thompson spoke up. "I heard it was a young, single French woman by the name of Simone Valinkofsky."

"Valinkofsky?" George repeated. "That doesn't sound very French."

"Well, I wouldn't know about that," Ms. Thompson replied. "But she moved in three days ago from what I hear. I haven't met her yet myself, but I understand that she has a very important job at the museum downtown."

"Interesting," I murmured. I knew better than to assume that the newcomer's recent arrival had anything to do with the zucchini situation. But I couldn't help noting that as far as I could determine so far, the vandalism had started the same day she'd moved into the neighborhood. Was it a connection, or merely a coincidence? Only further investigation would tell.

My friends and I finished our tea and then excused ourselves. We walked out the door, and made our way down the sidewalk. Mr. Geffington and Mrs. Mahoney both live on Bluff Street. I glanced at Mr. Geffington's house, a neat colonial with well-tended flower beds surrounding it. A set of concrete steps led down from the sidewalk to his curving front walk and the lush lawn that swept around the side of his house. In the backyard, I knew, lay Mr. Geffington's vegetable garden—along with the spectacular view of the river that all the homes on this side of the street shared.

Next I looked at Mr. Geffington's immediate neighbors. On the right side of his house was Mr. Safer's cozy-looking Tudor-style home. To the left was a small cottage-style house with a large front porch and an overgrown tangle of shrubs and vines peeking out of the backyard.

That would be a perfect place for someone to hide

out, I thought, my gaze wandering from the overgrown weed patch back to Mr. Geffington's yard. The two yards were separated only by a three-foot picket fence. Anyone who really wanted to could clear that easily.

Of course, opportunity wasn't the mystery here. The real mystery was motivation. What would make someone want to destroy a garden full of innocent zucchini? So far, I had no convincing theories about that.

George followed my glance. "The scene of the crime, eh?" she said. "Aren't you going to go over and dust for fingerprints on the eggplants or something?"

I gave her a playful shove. "Come on, let's see if the new neighbor is home."

All the yards on the river side of Bluff Street slope steeply down from the sidewalk. I stepped carefully down the stone steps in front of the former Peterson place. Leading the way across the narrow front yard onto the porch, I rang the bell.

The door opened a moment later, revealing a smiling young woman of about twenty-nine with shoulder-length dark hair and gorgeous black eyes. She was dressed simply but stylishly in a linen dress and chunky-heeled slides.

"Hello," she said in a soft, accented voice. "Can I help you?"

I introduced myself and my friends. Before I could

explain why we were there, the young woman gestured for us to enter.

"Please, come in," she urged. "My name is Simone Valinkofsky, and I have been hoping to meet some of my new neighbors."

Soon my friends and I were standing in the little house's surprisingly spacious living room. I had never been inside when the Petersons had lived there, but I suspected it hadn't looked anything like it did now. While there were still boxes here and there waiting to be unpacked, the new homeowner had already done much of the decorating in the room. A large oil painting hung over the fireplace, and tasteful curtains lined the large windows overlooking the backyard. Embossed books were set on built-in shelves on either side of the room, and several exotic ivory-handled fans were displayed on one wall. Bess stared openly at several gorgeous pieces of jewelry that decorated an end table.

"Wow," I commented, trying to take it all in. "You have a lot of cool stuff, Miss Valinkofsky."

"Please—call me Simone."

"Good," George said. "Because I'm not sure I could pronounce Valin—Valik—whatever. That sure wasn't in any of my high school French courses!"

Simone laughed, seeming surprised and delighted by George's frank comments. "No, it is not a French name," she said. "My great-grandfather fled to Paris from Russia during the revolution."

My gaze had just landed on an elaborate gold, jewel-encrusted orb in a glass display case with a lock on the mantel. "Did that come from Russia?" I asked, pointing it out.

Simone nodded. "Yes, you have a good eye," she replied. "That is a genuine Fabergé egg—the most prized heirloom of my family. It is not one of the world-famous imperial eggs that Fabergé made for the czars, of course. Most of those are in museums or elsewhere on display. But it is still quite a treasure, and we are all very proud of it, and of our Russian heritage."

She went on to describe several of the other unique and beautiful items in the room. It was so interesting that I almost forgot why we were there for a moment.

Finally Simone interrupted herself with a laugh. "But forgive me," she said. "I'm talking only about myself. Please, tell me more about you. What brought you to my doorstep today?"

"Nancy is a detective," Bess explained.

"Is that so?" Simone said in surprise. "But you are so young! I thought American detectives were old, gruff men like Humphrey Bogart, not pretty young girls."

I blushed. "I'm not a *real* detective," I explained quickly. "That is, I don't have a license or anything. I just help out my dad with some of his legal cases, stuff like that. For instance, today we're trying to figure out who has been going around and demolishing the zucchini in people's vegetable gardens."

"Zucchini?" Simone repeated.

"That's the American name for the vegetable you probably know as a *courgette*," George explained.

I shot her a surprised glance. Did George remember that random word from French class? But she's always coming up with odd trivia like this that she finds on the Internet—so maybe that's how she knew the word. Sometimes her quirky memory comes in very handy.

Simone laughed. "I see. Well, I'm afraid I can't be of any help," she said. "I've been so busy unpacking for the last three days that I've barely glanced out the window, let alone left the house. I can guarantee you it wasn't me, though. I would never demolish zucchini—I'd deep-fry it! And of course, I don't have a garden myself, so the culprit has had no reason to visit here."

I stepped toward the back windows, still looking around. When my gaze wandered toward the view outside, I gasped.

"Hey," I blurted out. "Isn't that a whole bunch of zucchini right there in your backyard?"

Party Plans

W hat? Where?" Simone sounded genuinely surprised as she hurried to join me at the window. Bess and George came over too, and all four of us stared out at the unkempt backyard. I pointed to several vigorous-looking vines twining their way over what appeared to be an overgrown rose hedge. Half a dozen oblong green fruits were growing from the vines.

"Hey! That does look like zucchini," George said.

"I think you may be right," Simone said. "As you can tell, we haven't had the chance to work on the yard much. Come, let's investigate."

My friends and I followed her through the kitchen into the backyard. Like the front yard, it sloped steeply down toward the drop-off over the river, which was lined by a low stone wall. About two-thirds of the way to the wall, the rose hedge blocked off at least half of the yard's width.

By standing on tiptoes, we could just see over the hedge into a vegetable garden gone wild. Tomato plants sprouted here and there, and spindly onion tops were already going to seed. The zucchini vines wound in and out around it all.

"Some of the seeds from last year's garden must have survived the winter and come back on their own," Bess commented. "Looks like you may be able to have your fried zucchini after all, Simone!"

"Yes, but only if I can find a way into the garden past all the thorns!" Simone said. "I'll have to ask Pierre to clear a path through them."

"Pierre?" I repeated curiously.

"You called?" a male voice responded cheerfully from directly behind me.

I jumped, startled. When I turned around, I found myself face-to-face with a handsome young man, perhaps ten years younger than Simone. There was a strong family resemblance to Simone in his dark eyes and high cheekbones.

"There you are, Pierre," Simone said. "Let me introduce you to my new friends—Nancy, Bess, and George. And this is Pierre, my nephew. He's from Paris too. He's staying with me for the summer until his university classes start up in Chicago."

19

Pierre gave a little bow. "Charmed," he said in a strong French accent, his gaze trained on Bess. "It's an honor to meet such lovely ladies."

George and I exchanged a quick glance and a knowing grin. We were used to seeing men go instantly gaga over our friend.

"I hope you're enjoying River Heights so far," Bess responded politely, returning Pierre's smile. "It's not the biggest town in the world, but there's a lot going on."

"*Oui,* like a zucchini bandit," Simone added with a smile. She gestured to one of the nearby vegetables. "It seems we are lucky to have some *courgettes* growing wild in the yard, Pierre. Someone is out to destroy all the rest of the zucchini in town."

"Yes." I checked my watch, realizing that it was getting late. I was supposed to meet my boyfriend, Ned Nickerson, for a movie date in a few hours. As much as I was enjoying the visit with Simone, I would have to move on soon if I wanted to do any further investigating today. "That reminds me, we should get going. And I'm sure you guys have lots to do."

Pierre looked slightly confused, but he continued to smile. "Ah, must you really fly off so soon?" He rested a hand on Bess's arm. "But please, *mesdemoiselles,* will you agree to return before long? In fact, some close friends of mine are coming from France to visit with me, and I know they would enjoy meeting you. Perhaps we could have a party once they are here?"

"A party?" George said, picking at one of the zucchini vines. "That sounds like fun. When are your friends arriving?"

Simone glanced at her watch. "Any moment now," she answered for her nephew. "They are driving in this afternoon from a bit farther down the river, where they were visiting some other friends. Perhaps we could all have a get-together this weekend—perhaps tomorrow night?"

I nodded. "That sounds great," I said. "Thank you!" I liked the idea of getting to know our new neighbors better. Even if Simone didn't know anything about the zucchini vandal, she was an interesting and likable person. I was eager to hear more about the exotic objects in her house, not to mention more details about her intriguing family history.

"Wonderful!" Pierre clapped his hands. "It's settled then. Shall we say seven o'clock tomorrow?"

"Sure," I said, and Bess and George nodded. "But now we really must be going. I need to meet my boyfriend soon."

"Oh, of course," Simone said. "And please feel free to bring him along tomorrow night. That goes for all of you." She smiled at the three of us.

"Indeed," Pierre added. "I'm sure such lovely girls as you must all have boyfriends, yes?"

Bess's dimples deepened. "Not quite," she said. "Nancy is the only one of us with a steady guy right now."

"Oh, that's too bad," Pierre said, though the words didn't sound terribly sincere. "Well, my friends and I will try to entertain you in any case."

"I'm sure you will." Bess returned the smile, batting her long eyelashes playfully as Pierre grinned in delight.

We all walked back toward the street. Instead of going through the house, we headed along the strip of lawn that separated the building from the low picket fence that marked Mr. Geffington's property line. I glanced over the fence curiously, wondering if I would spot any clues at the scene of the crime. But Mr. Geffington had long since cleared up the evidence. His garden looked as neat as could be, as usual.

I looked over my shoulder at the overgrown garden. Had someone hidden back there in the tangle and crept out to smash Mr. Geffington's zucchini at an opportune moment? Or had the culprit sneaked down the steep concrete steps from the street and scurried around the house under cover of darkness? Or had Mr. Safer merely had to step over from his own yard long enough to dispatch his neighbor's prized crop?

The last possibility still seemed hopelessly far-fetched. But a lifetime spent puzzling over mysteries has taught me never to discount any option, no matter how unlikely it seems. That's one of the things I like best about sleuthing—there's no way of guessing how any case is going to turn out until I've gathered all the evidence, followed all the leads, figured out all the clues.

When we reached the sidewalk, Bess and George and I bid our new friends farewell. As Simone and Pierre headed inside, the three of us walked toward Mr. Geffington's house.

"That Pierre seems like a nice guy, doesn't he?" Bess commented with a glance back at the house.

George snorted. "Sure, but I hope you send him your dry cleaning bill after the way he was drooling all over you."

Bess blushed. "Oh, stop it," she said. "He was just being friendly."

"Uh-huh," I said playfully. "And I'm sure you didn't even notice how cute he was. Or his cool French accent. Or the way he stared at you the whole time we were there."

"Whatever." Bess pointed to Mr. Geffington's house, which we were passing at the moment. "Hey, don't you want to stop in and look around or something? I mean, maybe it's all cleaned up now, but you might find some witnesses. Potatoes have eyes and corn has ears, you know."

I groaned loudly at the bad joke. Bess was obviously trying to change the subject, and I decided to let her. "No, I think we'd better go talk to Mr. Safer next," I said. "He's the prime suspect according to Mr. G. I'm sure he didn't do it, but maybe he saw or heard something that night that will give us a lead on the real culprit."

George shrugged. "Sounds like as good a plan as any," she said. "Just don't anyone ask if he's seen any good musicals lately, or we'll never get away."

We walked on to the steps leading down to Harold Safer's yard. Unlike the plain stone or concrete of most of the steps on the block, Mr. Safer's are decorated with bits of colored glass that form a rainbow pattern.

I led the way to the front door. When I pressed the doorbell, we could all hear the faint tune of "Somewhere over the Rainbow" ringing through the house.

Soon we also heard the sound of footsteps hurrying toward us. A moment later the door swung open—and there was Harold Safer, with a huge mallet in his hands.

A Call for Help

I gasped, startled by the unexpected sight. "What are you doing with that?" I blurted out, visions of smashed zucchini dancing through my head.

Harold Safer blinked, seeming confused by my reaction. "What am I doing with what?" he asked. Then he glanced down at the mallet. "Oh, you mean this? I was trying to hang up a curtain rod in the kitchen, but I seem to be all thumbs today." He sighed and rolled his eyes dramatically.

"You're trying to hang curtains with that?" Bess asked. "No wonder you're having trouble. Maybe I can help. Do you have a toolbox?"

Harold Safer looked surprised, but he gestured for us to come in. "It's in the basement," he told Bess.

She nodded. "Be right back." With that, she disappeared down the hall.

"Does she know what she's doing?" Harold Safer asked George and me, still looking surprised.

"Definitely," George assured him. "Bess is a wiz with tools—and I'm not just talking makeup brushes either."

I nodded. Most people are surprised to find out how handy Bess is. She looks like the sort of girl who would have trouble changing a lightbulb, but in fact she has an almost freakish natural ability to fix things, from a sticky toaster to a stalled car. A simple curtain rod would be a piece of cake for her.

"Don't worry, Mr. Safer," I added. "She'll have the job done in no time."

Harold Safer sighed. "Well, I'm glad she's here, then," he said, leading the way toward the kitchen at the back of his house. "If I don't get that curtain hung soon, I'm going to go crazy. I thought this would only take a minute; I have to get back to my shop. Plus, that nutjob neighbor of mine keeps glaring at me from next door every time I go in my kitchen. Can you believe that? Just because someone decides to mess with his garden, he thinks I'm responsible. You should have seen him last night—he was out there weeding, and he shot me so many dirty looks I wanted to go take a bath!"

We entered the kitchen. It was clean and spacious, the white walls decorated with framed posters from various Broadway shows. Large windows overlooked the back and side yards. Lying on the floor below the side window were a shiny brass curtain rod, a set of linen curtains, several bent nails, and a small pile of dust.

"Yes, we heard about the zucchini problem," I said. "That's why we're here, actually. We want to find out who really did it."

"Really? Good," Harold Safer said, flopping down onto a barstool at the counter. "Because at this point I'm afraid to go outside!"

I could tell he was being dramatic, but his comments reminded me that I needed to take this mystery seriously, even if my friends wouldn't. Neighborly relations were at stake. If Mr. Safer was hanging a curtain that would block even a part of his precious view just because of Mr. Geffington, things had to be pretty bad.

Just then Bess entered holding a small hammer and some other tools. "Here we go," she said cheerfully. "This should work much better than that mallet. Come on, George, help me hold up the brackets."

As the cousins got to work, I sat down next to Harold Safer at the counter. "Do you mind answering a few questions?" I asked him.

He shrugged. "Ask away, Nancy," he said. "I have

nothing to hide from you or anybody else, no matter what that close-minded, zucchini-obsessed neighbor of mine says to the contrary. I mean, his accusations were actually sort of amusing at first. Can you imagine *me* sneaking into his garden in the dead of night, wielding some sort of caveman club, and smashing away at his precious vegetables? Although it *does* bring to mind that old joke: What do you get when an elephant walks through your garden?"

"What?" I asked.

"Squash!" He grinned with delight.

"All right, then," I said with a polite chuckle. I could see that, as usual, it was going to be difficult to get a word in edgewise once Mr. Safer started talking. "Did you see or hear anything unusual on Tuesday night?"

"Not a thing." He shrugged. "As I recall, I went inside that night after the sunset and listened to the cast recording of *Fiddler on the Roof.* It's one of my favorites, so I had it turned up quite loud. In fact, I almost didn't hear the doorbell when Mrs. Zucker and little Owen stopped by after dinner, collecting for the Anvil Day festivities. So naturally I wouldn't have heard anything going on next door short of a cannon blast."

"I see," I said. "And did you see the damage the next day? To the zucchini, I mean."

"No," he replied. "As you know, I don't open the

shop until ten A.M., and I don't get up much before nine most mornings. By the time I looked out the window, I suppose Bradley had already cleared up the mess. At least, I never noticed a thing—didn't even know what had happened until he came ranting and raving into the shop later that day."

"He came into the cheese shop and accused you?" I asked.

"Yes, can you imagine the nerve?" Mr. Safer looked insulted. "Luckily there were no customers in there at the time. Once I figured out what he was going on about, I told him I didn't do it. But he just muttered something about taking legal action and stormed out. I can't imagine why he thought I would do such a thing!"

"I guess he thought you were mad about his tomato cages blocking your view," I said.

"What?" He looked honestly surprised. "Are you serious? But that's so last month's news! Once I realized he wasn't going to move those cages—why *do* they have to be so tall, anyway? You'd think he wanted his tomatoes to try out for a revival of *Little Shop of Horrors* or something—I simply moved my chaise a few yards to the right, and *voila*! Uninterrupted sunset views once again."

I blinked, trying to unwind his convoluted comments. "I see," I said, when I finally figured out what he had just said. "Well, that's all I can think of right now, then. I guess I'll have to keep asking around and see if anyone else witnessed anything that night."

Harold Safer nodded. "Have you checked in with the people on the other side?" he asked. "I hear a young lady moved in earlier this week. I haven't met her yet myself, but I'm dying to. I heard she's the daughter of a fabulously wealthy European jet-setter. Possibly even some sort of minor royalty. Can you imagine? Right here in little old River Heights!"

"We just met her," I said. "Her name is Simone, and she's very nice. But she didn't say anything about royalty or the rest of it. She also didn't see anything happen at Mr. Geffington's the other night."

"Too bad," Harold Safer said. "Ah well, I keep telling that insufferable Geffington that it was probably just raccoons after his zucchini anyway. Of course, he keeps insisting that it couldn't have been, unless raccoons have learned to wield sledgehammers." He rolled his eyes.

I smiled sympathetically and glanced over at Bess and George, who were sliding the curtain rod into its newly hung brackets. At that moment Mr. Safer looked over and noticed what they were doing too.

"Oh, wonderful!" he exclaimed, clapping his hands and jumping to his feet. "You girls are geniuses. I can't thank you enough. You've saved my sanity, such as it is."

"It was no trouble at all, Mr. Safer," Bess replied. "We'd better get going."

"I won't hear of it! At least let me thank you girls with nice, cold sodas." He was already hurrying toward the refrigerator. "Now, I won't take no for an answer! Besides, I simply must tell someone about the revival of *A Chorus Line* I caught down in River City last weekend. . . ."

I exchanged a glance with Bess and George. Obviously we weren't going to be able to make a clean break of it this time. But I didn't really mind. Sitting quietly while Harold Safer rambled on about his latest theater experience would give me a chance to think about the case.

And I was starting to realize that this case really would take some thought. It might seem trivial on the surface, but that didn't mean it was going to be easy to solve. So far I'd turned up no witnesses, no clues, no motive, and no real direction for the investigation. On top of that, the scene of the crime had long since been cleared of any evidence that might have been there. How was I supposed to track down what had happened with absolutely nothing to go on?

The clues are there, I reminded myself, as Mr. Safer served us sodas and chattered on happily. They always are. You just have to find them.

That made me feel a little better. I sipped at my soda, going over what I'd learned so far. It wasn't much. But it was a start.

It was hard to stop Mr. Safer once he'd started talking. After describing the play he'd seen in astounding detail, he insisted on sharing the latest photos he'd taken of the sun setting over the river. Then he wanted us to listen to a new cast recording he'd downloaded off the Internet. George was actually sort of interested in that, though only the downloading part. She loves talking about computers with anyone who shares her passion for them, especially since Bess and I aren't interested in them much beyond checking our e-mail or doing a little occasional research.

Finally we managed to make our escape. Mr. Safer walked us to the door. "Thanks so much for stopping by, girls," he said cheerfully. "I truly appreciate the help with the curtains. Not to mention your interest in the whole messy zucchini situation. If anyone can get to the bottom of this, it's our own River Heights supersleuth, Nancy Drew." He winked at me. "One of these days I'm going to write a musical about you, my dear!"

I smiled. Mr. Safer has been saying that same thing since the first time I appeared in the newspaper for cracking a tough case. "Thanks for all your help, Mr. Safer," I said. "I'll be in touch."

Soon Bess, George, and I were hurrying down the sidewalk toward my house. "I wish we had time to talk to a few more people today," I commented, glancing at my watch. "Talking to Mr. Safer has made me realize it really would be better to clear this up sooner rather than later."

"Yeah, I see your point," George admitted. "Mr. Safer seemed pretty freaked out about all this."

Bess nodded. "He and Mr. Geffington have had disagreements before, but nothing like this. We've got to do something before things go any further."

"I'm supposed to meet Ned in an hour to go to the movies," I said as we reached the sidewalk in front of my house. We all paused in front of Bess's car, which was parked at the curb. "But maybe we can pick up on this sometime over the weekend if you guys aren't busy."

"Sure," Bess agreed for both of them. "Oh, and if you're going out with Ned, you should wear that lavender blouse you never wear. It really brings out the color of your eyes. And don't forget to put on lipstick! I keep telling you, it really makes a difference."

Bess is always trying to convince both George and

33

me to take more interest in clothes and makeup—two subjects that interest her a lot and us not much at all. I like an occasional shopping spree as much as the next girl, and I enjoy wearing nice things on special occasions, but most of the time I just can't be bothered thinking too much about stuff like that. As for George, she's been a tomboy since the day she was born. If Bess hasn't turned her into a fashion fiend by now, I don't think it's ever going to happen.

"Okay, I'll attempt to look human if at all possible," I told Bess, with a playful wink at George. "See you guys tomorrow."

We parted ways, and I hurried into the house. Dad was nowhere to be seen, but our housekeeper, Hannah Gruen, was fixing dinner in the kitchen. Hannah has been with us since my mother died, and I think of her as part of the family. She appears brisk and efficient on the outside, but underneath her no-nonsense exterior lies a heart as ample as her considerable girth.

"Oh, there you are, Nancy," Hannah said, wiping her hands on her apron. "You just missed a phone call. The young lady sounded rather upset! Her number is on the pad."

"Thanks." I hurried to look at the notepad next to the phone. Simone's name and phone number were written there in Hannah's neat cursive. "Oh! That's the new owner of the Peterson place. We met her this afternoon. I wonder what she wants?"

Figuring there was only one way to find out, I dialed the number. Simone answered, though she sounded so upset that I almost didn't recognize her voice. "Nancy!" she cried when I identified myself. "I am so glad to hear from you. As you know, Pierre and I have met almost no one here in River Heights yet, and I didn't know where else to turn."

"What is it, Simone?" I asked anxiously. The worried crackle in her voice told me that something was wrong—very wrong.

"It's my Fabergé egg," Simone replied. "I walked into the living room and noticed that it's gone!"

A Stolen Heirloom

F **ive minutes later I** was back on Simone's porch, ringing her doorbell. When Simone answered the door, her face looked flushed and she was frowning.

"Oh! It's you," she said, her scowl fading slightly. "Come in, Nancy. I thought you might be the police. I called them right before I called you."

"I'm sure they'll be here soon," I said tactfully. I decided it wouldn't help anyone to mention that Chief McGinnis of the River Heights Police Department doesn't always bother to hurry unless the crime is something that might land him a headline in the Chicago papers. "In the meantime, do you want to tell me what happened?"

"Of course." Simone gestured for me to follow her

inside. "Come in, I'll introduce you to Pierre's friends. They can help me explain it all."

I followed her into the living room. It didn't look much like a crime scene. Having been there just a few hours earlier, I didn't notice anything out of place.

With one exception, of course. The glass case on the mantel that had held the Fabergé egg was open and empty.

"You didn't clean things up after you found the egg missing, did you?" I asked.

Simone shook her head. "We haven't touched a thing," she said. "The egg seems to be the only thing that interested the burglar. Nothing else in here appears to have been disturbed."

"Interesting," I said.

At that moment I heard voices from the direction of the kitchen. Pierre walked into the room, followed by three other young men.

"Nancy!" Pierre exclaimed as soon as he spotted me. "I'm so glad you are here. Please allow me to introduce my friends: This is Jacques, and Thèo, and René."

He gestured to each young man in turn. Jacques was tall and slender, with light brown hair and an attractive face that had a slightly melancholy expression. Thèo was shorter, with dark hair and broad shoulders. René had sparkling green eyes, and hair as dark as Thèo's but much curlier.

"Nice to meet you all," I said as the boys greeted me politely. "Welcome to River Heights. Sorry you had to arrive at such an unfortunate moment."

"Actually, they had already been here a little while when it happened," Simone said. "They arrived just a few minutes after you and your friends left."

"Yes, and we feel just awful about it all, as we feel we are partly responsible," Jacques said earnestly in lightly accented English.

"What do you mean?" I asked.

Thèo shrugged. "It is because we forgot to lock the door." His French accent was much stronger than Jacques's, but his voice and expression were equally worried. "Pierre, he offered to show us the town. We were all very eager to see it, and so we hardly took the time to put our luggage upstairs or lock the doors."

"Yes, it's my fault." Pierre sighed loudly. "Simone, she is always telling me to lock the doors. It may be a small town, but there are bad people everywhere. But I just cannot remember. This town—after Paris, it seems so . . . so *good*."

I sighed. "Trust me, we get our share of crime even here in sleepy little River Heights." Sometimes it seems we get much more than our share, in fact. But

I didn't bother to try to explain that. Simone, Pierre, and their friends already felt bad enough.

"Well, I shouldn't have left you all here so soon after your arrival," Simone said. "I was just so eager to get the supplies for our party tomorrow night. I didn't want to put off the shopping too long."

The French guys all spoke up at once, reassuring Simone that she was in no way responsible and that the fault was all theirs. Meanwhile, I looked around the room more carefully. I stepped toward the fireplace, being careful not to touch or bump into anything. The last thing I wanted to do was mess up the crime scene before the police arrived. But I was still having trouble believing that nothing else had been touched.

"These bracelets," I spoke up abruptly, interrupting whatever the others were saying. I pointed to the jeweled pieces that Bess had admired earlier. They were lying on an end table along with a few other knickknacks. "Simone, they look valuable. Are they?"

"Oh, yes, I suppose so," Simone replied. "I mean, those are real diamonds and pearls, so they must be worth a little something. They have sentimental family value to me; that's why I display them here."

"Why wouldn't the thief grab something like that on the way past?" I whispered, speaking more to myself than to the others. "It would be easy enough to slip them in a pocket or something. . . ." I glanced around and saw other valuable items—figurines, oil paintings, glassware, and more. Why only take the egg?

"That is a good question," René said, having heard my comments. "Perhaps we startled the thief upon our return."

"When did you return, exactly?" I asked. "Please, could you tell me everything that happened—how long you were out, when you discovered the theft, and so on?"

"Well, of course," Pierre said, though he looked surprised at the request. I guessed that meant that Simone hadn't told him about my reputation as a detective. "My friends arrived about fifteen minutes after you left, as Simone said. We showed them around the house, then Simone left almost immediately to do the shopping. My friends took their bags upstairs, then we went out to walk around the neighborhood. We were gone about an hour, maybe a little more. When Jacques and René returned to the house together, Simone had just come in and noticed the egg missing. Thèo and I were still outside looking at the river, and we rushed in when René called us, and then heard what had happened."

"That's right," Simone said. "I noticed that the egg was gone right away, because the sun was slanting in through the window and hit the open door of the case to make a reflection."

"I see." I thought about that for a moment. "And was the case locked before?"

"Yes," Simone said. "And the case is bolted to the wall. But it wouldn't have been difficult for the thief to find the key. I only kept it tucked under the clock there." She pointed to a clock sitting on the other end of the mantel.

I stepped a little closer to the fireplace for a better look at the clock. As I did so, the adjoining den came into view through an open doorway. I saw that a table in there was overturned.

"Did the thief do that as well?" I asked, pointing.

Pierre nodded. "He must have," he said. "See? The table was near the back door. We think he heard us coming back from our walk and in his rush to get out he knocked into the table."

"Yes, and if René didn't always talk so much, perhaps we would have heard the crash," Thèo added with a twinkle in his eye.

Jacques frowned slightly at him. "It is not a time for jokes, Thèo," he said mildly. "Our friends have lost a valuable family treasure. That egg has been with them for generations, you know."

"Yes, I know." Thèo looked chagrined. "My apologies, Simone and Pierre."

"No apology is necessary, Thèo," Simone said. "It was only an object that was taken. At least no one was here when the thief came, or someone might have been hurt. That would have been much, much worse."

She sighed, looking sad and hopeless. "Don't worry," I told her quietly, stepping closer as the guys started talking among themselves. "I'll help you find your egg if I can."

"You think you can find it?" Simone looked surprised. "Oh, Nancy, I know you said earlier that you are a detective. But this . . . How could you hope to do such a thing? I'm not sure even the police will be able to help me. There are so many places for such an item to disappear quickly. . . ." She sighed again.

I knew she had a point. If a professional thief had taken the Fabergé egg, it surely would be well on its way to some sort of black-market art auction by now. But my little sixth sense was tingling, and that made me think that I needed to do some more investigating to get the answers to some questions. For one thing, how would a professional art thief even know about Simone's egg? And why would such a person leave behind other items he could easily sell as well? It just didn't make sense. And when something doesn't make sense, I've learned that usually means there's more to the story than meets the eye.

"Don't worry," I told her again. "I think there's still a chance we could get your egg back."

I noticed that Jacques had turned away from the other guys and was listening to me. He looked surprised too, but didn't say anything, and he quickly turned away again.

Meanwhile Simone smiled at me, though she still didn't look terribly hopeful. "I wonder what could be keeping the police?" she commented, glancing at her watch. "I called them nearly an hour ago. . . ."

"An hour?" I gulped, suddenly realizing how much time had passed. Looking at my own watch, I realized I was in trouble. "Uh-oh," I said. "I was supposed to meet my boyfriend ten minutes ago! I've got to go."

"I'm sorry! Ned, I'm so, so sorry!" I exclaimed breathlessly as I raced into the lobby of the River Heights cineplex. It wasn't hard to spot my boyfriend, Ned Nickerson—he was the only one in the lobby other than the ticket taker and the teenage girl working at the popcorn stand. That was no surprise, since the movie we'd planned to see had been scheduled to start ten minutes earlier.

Ned smiled, displaying his adorable dimples, as he stood up from one of the lobby's padded benches to greet me. "It's okay," he said, running one hand over his brown hair. His brown eyes twinkled playfully. "I figured that whatever was keeping you was probably more interesting than the movie anyway . . . or your name isn't Nancy Drew."

I laughed. "Actually, you're right about that," I said. "I'll tell you all about it. Since we already missed the beginning of the movie, can I buy you dinner instead?"

"Absolutely!" Ned said immediately, despite the empty popcorn tub sitting on the bench beside him. That's one of the predictable things about Ned: In addition to being patient and understanding, he's always ready to eat. He and George are a lot alike that way. Like George, Ned's love of food never seems to affect his tall, lanky frame too much, even though Hannah likes to say that he eats enough to feed a small army.

We left the theater and headed down the block to one of our favorite places to eat, a combination bookstore and café called Susie's Read & Feed. Tucked into a tall, narrow storefront on River Street between a clothing store and the First Bank of River Heights, Susie's is a cramped but wonderful place, every inch of the walls lined with tall bookcases crammed with an eclectic variety of reading material, and every inch of space in between is occupied by mismatched, brightly painted wooden tables and chairs. The owner, a tiny, energetic young woman named Susie Lin, keeps both the books and the food varied and interesting, which has made the place very popular with locals of all ages.

Luckily we'd arrived early enough that it wasn't too crowded, and we soon found a free table in the General Nonfiction section. I could see Ned scanning the titles on the shelves as we sat down. He loves to read anything and everything he can get his hands on, and is always looking for new material.

But instead of grabbing a book, he turned his attention to me. "Let's hear it," he said simply. "I can tell you're on the trail of something especially interesting. And not just because you were late."

"Really? What do you mean?" I asked in surprise.

Instead of answering, he merely pointed at me. I glanced down and belatedly realized that I was still wearing the same clothes I'd had on all day. In my great hurry to get to the movie theater from Simone's house, I hadn't ever gotten around to changing for my date.

But unlike Bess, Ned isn't one to notice clothes too much. So I knew that probably wasn't what he was talking about.

I put my hand to my hair, wondering if it was that obvious that I hadn't brushed it since that morning. My fingers encountered something oddly hard and prickly up there.

"Ugh!" I exclaimed, yanking at the strange object.

It turned out to be a short, thorny branch—probably a piece of wild rose cane that had gotten into my hair while I was peering into Simone's overgrown garden from the rose hedge earlier in the afternoon. I was a little surprised that Bess hadn't noticed and removed it for me, but not at all surprised that I hadn't noticed it myself. I'd had a lot more interesting things on my mind all afternoon than my own hair.

Ned grinned. "Either Bess convinced you to try some really weird new fashion statement, or you're so distracted by some exciting new mystery that you haven't bothered to glance in the mirror lately."

"Guilty on the second count," I admitted, quickly running my hands over my hair to check for any more stray debris. "Let's order something to eat, and then I'll tell you all about it."

Ned nodded. At that moment Susie Lin hurried toward our table with her order pad in hand. Not only is she the head cook, but the main waitress as well.

I glanced at the chalkboard propped up over the cash register, where Susie always writes the daily specials. One of the entrées caught my eye immediately: zucchini fritters.

"Oh!" I said, suddenly remembering the other mystery I was supposed to be investigating. In all the excitement over the theft at Simone's house, I had nearly forgotten about the vegetable vandal for the moment. But now I wondered if there could possibly be any connection between the two cases. Hadn't I already noted the odd coincidence of the zucchini smasher turning up in town on the same day that Simone and Pierre had moved in?

"Hi, Nancy, Ned." Susie greeted us in her usual quick, clipped voice. "What can I get you this evening?"

Susie is one of those people who never seems to stop moving. She sometimes reminds me of the ball in a pinball machine as she bounces from one end of her long, narrow restaurant to the other, taking orders, bringing food, and clambering up the rolling ladders set into tracks in the bookcases to fetch books for people from the higher shelves.

"The shrimp enchiladas sound good, don't they, Nancy?" Ned commented as he looked over at the Specials board.

"They do sound yummy," I agreed. "But I think I'm going to try the zucchini fritters."

Susie's eyes widened, and she flung up her hands so violently that the pen she was holding went flying. "Zucchini?" she exclaimed. "Please, don't even *talk* to me about zucchini!"

5

Leads and Clues

I was startled by Susie's violent reaction. Had she been a victim of the zucchini smasher, too? Maybe I had been too quick to categorize that case as merely a pesky problem between neighbors.

"Wait," I said quickly, ignoring Ned's surprised look. "Have you been having, uh, zucchini-related problems lately?"

Susie sighed loudly, pushing back a strand of her long, straight black hair. "Aye-yie-yie, I'm sorry, Nancy," she said. "It's been a long day. And yes, part of the reason has to do with zucchini, believe it or not."

"What do you mean?" My mind was racing, already imagining some sort of vast zucchini conspiracy. But I forced such thoughts out of my head as I listened to Susie's answer. Better to keep an open mind and work from the facts, not jump to conclusions.

"It all started at lunchtime yesterday, when I was writing up the dinner menu for the next couple of days." Susie gestured toward the Specials board. "I'd just written down the zucchini fritters when Bradley Geffington came in. You know him, don't you? He manages the bank next door."

"Of course," I said, and Ned nodded, although Susie's question was probably mostly rhetorical. In a small city like River Heights, practically everyone knows everyone else.

"Bradley comes in here a lot for lunch," Susie went on, leaning on the table as she talked. "In fact, he usually takes his break early so he can get here before it gets crowded—and before we run out of cheese biscuits."

Ned smiled appreciatively and nodded. Susie's cheese biscuits are legendary.

"So yesterday he was a little later than normal. The place was packed, so he stopped near the counter to look for a table. He saw what I was doing—like I said, I was writing up the dinner board and I'd just written down the zucchini fritters. Well, you would have thought I'd written that I would be serving live squirrels with cyanide sauce for dinner!" Susie looked annoyed as she recalled what had happened. "Bradley started ranting and raving. At first I thought he was angry because there were no free tables or something. But he kept saying zucchini this, zucchini that—I still don't know what he was going on about, because a moment later Harold Safer from the cheese shop came in. The two of them started arguing and yelling at each other until I was afraid one of them was going to take a swing at the other. I finally had to kick them both out so they wouldn't scare off my other customers."

"Weird," Ned commented. "I thought those two were pretty good friends. They live right next door to each other."

I had to agree that there was something weird about what Susie had just said. Why hadn't Mr. Safer mentioned running into Mr. Geffington when I'd talked with him earlier? Had he simply forgotten, or had he kept the encounter from me on purpose?

"But that's not all," Susie continued, rolling her eyes. "I was still trying to figure that one out a couple of hours later, when some woman I didn't know with a French accent came in. She's having some kind of party tomorrow night, and she wanted to order a bunch of my baked goods and canapés and stuff for it. When she saw the zucchini fritters on the menu, she started babbling about *courgettes* and gardens, and insisted on buying up as many fritters as I could make for her right then." She shrugged. "I told her they'd probably be a little stale by tomorrow night, but she wouldn't take no for an answer."

"That was Simone Valinkofsky," I told Susie as Ned shot me another surprised glance. "She just bought the Peterson place on Bluff Street."

"Well, I guess the fritters were popular, because right after she left with my whole supply, three or four other customers came in wanting to order some. Seems they'd heard about them from people who'd tried them at lunch. And on top of that, I had the usual run of little kids looking at the menu and yelling about how zucchini tastes like boogers! The worst were those loud Callahan twins and their little friend Owen. The three of them carried on until their mothers dragged them out without ordering." She sighed loudly. "I know, it sounds silly to complain about this. It just seems like everyone in town is suddenly getting weird about zucchini."

"Tell me about it," I muttered under my breath, though I couldn't help smiling at Susie's story about the zucchini-hating little kids.

After her tirade, Susie seemed to feel much better. "Anyway, there are no zucchini fritters left," she told Ned and me. "But the enchiladas are excellent tonight, if I do say so myself."

"Great. We'll take two orders," Ned said, glancing over at me. I nodded, and Susie rushed off toward the kitchen.

Tapping my fingers on the table, I stared at the top shelf of the bookcase across the way, though I wasn't really seeing the rows of books about animals and pet care. I was thinking about the zucchini case. Did anything Susie had just said have anything to do with the vegetable vandal, or was the zucchini connection just a coincidence? I wasn't sure yet, though that sixth sense of mine was tingling again.

Suddenly I noticed that Ned was staring at me, smiling his familiar patient smile.

"So, are you going to tell me what's going on?" he inquired, arching one eyebrow at me. "Or do I have to wait and read about it in the paper like everyone else in River Heights?"

I giggled. "Sorry. Brain in overdrive," I apologized. "Believe it or not, *two* cases turned up this afternoon."

I quickly filled him in on the zucchini smasher and then on Simone's robbery. Ned listened intently, not saying much until I was finished. Then he leaned back in his chair. "Weird," he said. "Any theories yet on who's behind either crime?"

"Well, the zucchini case suddenly seems to have plenty of leads and clues now that everyone is talking about zucchini. But no one has any real motive," I replied. "And the Fabergé egg case has an obvious motivation: That egg has to be worth a ton. But there are no clues or leads. Really, almost anyone in town could have committed either crime. The door to Simone's house was wide open when the egg was taken, and of course Mr. Geffington's garden isn't exactly Fort Knox either. In both cases, it's a matter of good timing."

"Good point," Ned said. "But the right timing can be a tricky thing. Even in the middle of the night, someone might have looked out the window and seen whoever it was out there in the garden bashing vegetables. And the egg thief was taking an even bigger chance, sneaking into that house in broad daylight. He could have no way of knowing whether someone might return at any moment and catch him."

"Right. In fact, the French guys think that almost happened." I furrowed my brow. Something about what Ned had just said made me think of something else. "Unless, of course, that person *did* know just where everyone was. Or wasn't worried about being caught in the house."

"What do you mean?" Ned played with his fork, tapping it softly on his water glass. "Are you thinking it was an inside job?" Ned's not into mysteries in the same way I am, but he's more than smart enough to follow along when I'm in full hypothesizing mode.

"Maybe," I said. "The guys never actually said that they all returned at the same time from their tour of the neighborhood. In fact, they said something about a couple of them going inside—Jacques and René, I think it was—while the other two were still outside. And of course, Simone beat them all home according to what they told me." It was hard to imagine nice, friendly, intelligent Simone being the thief. But stranger things had happened. If the egg was insured, she would get a lot of money for its loss.

"Of course, it still might have been an outsider who just saw an opportunity and went for it," Ned commented. "But it sounds like you need to talk to Simone and the guys a little more."

"Definitely," I agreed. "I'm not ruling out the passing stranger thing yet, but it's just too coincidental that Pierre's friends all turned up about an hour or two before the egg was stolen. I'm glad I'll have the chance to talk with them and observe them tomorrow night at the party."

"Party?" Ned repeated, as I belatedly realized I'd forgotten to tell him about the get-together.

Before I could fill him in, though, another voice spoke up from just behind my right shoulder.

"Party? What party?"

6

Messy Motives

I glanced up and saw a pretty, dark-haired girl standing behind me. I sighed.

"Hello, Deirdre," I said.

Deirdre Shannon is my age, and her father is also a very successful local attorney. And we've known each other forever. Aside from that, the two of us don't have a whole lot in common. I always like to see the best in people, even the criminals I catch. But there's not much *best* to see in Deirdre as far as I can tell— although Bess would probably suggest *best dressed*. Since Deirdre seems to care more about her wardrobe than she does about most people, she would probably take that as a compliment.

Now she was standing there at our table, completely blocking the aisle of the cramped restaurant and smiling flirtatiously at Ned as if Generic Boyfriend #37 wasn't standing right there next to her. Deirdre seems to have a new guy on her arm every time I see her, so it would be a waste of time trying to keep track of the specifics.

"Nancy," Deirdre responded coldly. Then she turned a brilliant smile in Ned's direction. "Hey there, Ned. Did I hear you say you're going to a party this weekend? Anything fun I should know about?"

Ned shrugged. "Sorry, Deirdre, it's not really that kind of party," he said politely. "It's just a get-together for some of Nancy's new neighbors."

"Oh." Deirdre looked decidedly disinterested. Then her expression brightened. "Wait, you're not talking about the new French girl I've been hearing so much about, are you?"

"Simone is French, yes," I said. "What have you been hearing?" Normally I don't like to listen to Deirdre's gossip, since it's usually either completely trivial or wildly inaccurate. But she does know a lot of people, and once in a while she actually turns up some useful information. A good detective has to look for clues wherever she can find them.

Generic Boyfriend #37 cleared his throat. "I think there's a free table over there, Deirdre," he said.

"In a minute," Deirdre replied with impatience, not even bothering to glance in his direction. She leaned on the table, so close to Ned that the filmy sleeve of her silk blouse brushed his arm. "Well, this is just a rumor of course," she said eagerly, lowering her voice slightly. "But I heard that the reason she left France was because the government kicked her out for being mentally unstable and a danger to the public good."

"What?" I said skeptically. "I haven't heard of anything like that."

Deirdre shrugged and flipped her dark curls behind her shoulder. "Believe it or not, there are a few things in the world even *you* haven't heard of, Nancy Drew," she said. "Anyway, you asked what I'd heard and I'm telling you. What do you want from me?"

"Fine, okay, go on," I said soothingly, hoping to avoid a patent Deirdre Shannon public meltdown. In addition to her other charming qualities, she has a temper like an overcaffeinated Chihuahua. "Anything else?"

"Oh, I don't know." Deirdre seemed to be losing interest. "There was something about the Russian Mafia, but I think that was just speculation."

As opposed to the rest of your meticulously verified facts, I thought, though I didn't say it aloud. Deirdre doesn't deal too well with sarcasm.

"Deirdre," Generic Boyfriend #37 broke in again, sounding more impatient this time. "Come on, aren't we going to sit down? I'm starving."

Deirdre blew out a loud sigh and rolled her eyes. "Fine, whatever," she snapped. "Let's go sit down." With one last smile for Ned, she tossed her hair and turned away.

As soon as Deirdre and her date were seated well out of earshot, Ned grinned at me. "Good to see that her long, unbroken record of useless and petty gossip still stands," he joked.

"Yep. Along with her long, unbroken crush on you," I teased.

Ned pretended to flex his biceps. "Hey, what can I say? I'm just that irresistible," he teased back.

I giggled. Deirdre has had a monster crush on Ned since we were all in junior high. It's become sort of a running joke among my friends.

Then my expression sobered. "You don't think there could really be any truth to what she said, do you?"

"You mean about the Russian Mafia?" Ned said, taking a sip of his water. "I don't know, but what difference does it make, unless they've moved their headquarters to River Heights and put out a hit on all the city's zucchini?"

"No, not that part. The other stuff. About Simone being mentally unstable. Not that I think she really would have been kicked out of France for that, but—"

"But you're wondering if there's a kernel of truth in the story," Ned finished for me.

I smiled at him. "Exactly. I mean, Simone is so sweet, I hate to think badly of her. But maybe I should keep an extra close eye on her at that party."

That reminded me that I still hadn't told him about the party. I filled him in, and he promised to come with me. Then, as we spotted Susie Lin heading our way with a trayful of food, we put all mysteries aside and focused our minds on digging in.

For a few hours the next morning I almost forgot about both of the mysteries I was trying to solve. The River Heights Animal Shelter where I volunteer one morning a month is always busy on Saturdays, but today it was chaotic. People come from all over the city and the surrounding counties to adopt dogs and cats and the occasional rabbit or guinea pig. All morning I was running around and filling out paperwork, scrubbing cat cages, hosing down dog runs, and answering people's questions. There was no time to think about anything else.

But as soon as I headed toward home, the previous day's events came flooding back into my mind. Simone's party didn't start for about six hours, and I didn't want to wait that long to get back to my investigation.

I found Hannah in the kitchen, scrubbing out a saucepan in the sink. "Hi, Nancy," she greeted me, turning and wiping her hands on a dish towel. "How was the shelter today?"

"Fine," I replied. "We adopted out eleven cats and seven and a half dogs."

"Seven and a half?" Hannah repeated in surprise.

I smiled. "The Harrison family picked out the dog they want, but they're going away for a couple of days next week. So they're going to pick up their new pooch next weekend."

"Ah, that sounds nice," Hannah said. "I made some chili with the tomatoes and beans Evaline Waters gave us from her garden. Would you like a bowl for lunch?"

"Sure, thanks, Hannah. That sounds great."

I walked to the cabinet to grab a glass while Hannah pulled a tureen out of the refrigerator. A few minutes later I was seated at the round oak kitchen table with a bowl of hot chili and a cold glass of milk.

"Aren't you going to eat?" I asked Hannah.

She slid the tureen back into the refrigerator and turned back to face me. "I already had a bite earlier with your father," she said. "He had a meeting downtown this afternoon, so we had an early lunch before he left."

"Oh." I was a little disappointed to hear that Dad wasn't home. I had been hoping to talk over my cases with him. Scooping up a hot spoonful of chili, I blew on it before putting it in my mouth. Yum. "Mm, this chili is delicious, Hannah!" I took another bite. "Did anyone call this morning while I was out?"

"Just Bess," Hannah said. "She wants you to call her. Something about dressing for a party? I think she's planning to come by, and she wanted to know what time you'd be home."

"Okay, thanks." I told Hannah about the party so she wouldn't hold dinner for me. As she bustled off to take care of the laundry, I finished my lunch and put the dishes in the dishwasher. After that I wandered out into the hall, wondering what to do next.

I glanced at my watch. Still several hours until party time. I was counting on figuring out a lot at that party, but that didn't mean I was going to let the rest of the afternoon go to waste.

Heading into the living room, I picked up the phone and dialed a familiar number. It rang only once.

"Hello," a crisp female voice said. "River Heights Police Department. How may I help you?"

"Hi, Tonya," I said. "It's Nancy Drew."

"Oh, hello, Nancy. What can I do for you today?" Tonya Ward is the receptionist at police headquarters. She's efficient, smart, and tough. She's also a very helpful friend for me to have, since her boss, Chief McGinnis, isn't always thrilled to find out about my amateur investigating.

"Is the chief in?" I asked.

"Hold on a sec, I'll find out."

The line went quiet for a moment or two. Then it clicked back on, and a different voice spoke. "Hello?"

"Hi, Chief McGinnis," I said. "It's Nancy Drew."

"Yes, I heard." The chief sounded slightly weary. "What is it, Nancy?"

I switched the phone to my other ear and picked up a pen in case I needed to take any notes. "I was just wondering if you'd turned up anything in the Valinkofsky case during your investigation yesterday."

"Yes, I heard you beat us to the crime scene," the chief said dryly. He didn't add the word *again,* but I could tell he was thinking it. It was time for me to be extra tactful.

"Well, as you know, Simone only lives a couple of blocks from me," I said brightly. "I just went over to give her some moral support, really."

"Mm-hmm." The chief didn't sound convinced.

I cleared my throat. "Anyway, I did take a quick look around. But there really didn't seem to be any obvious clues. I mean, the house was unlocked and the key to the glass case was right there almost in plain sight. So unless there were any fingerprints or anything . . ."

"Okay, okay," Chief McGinnis said with a sigh. "I can take a hint, Nancy. No, we didn't find any unusual prints anywhere in the room. Just those of Ms.

Valinkofsky and her houseguests. Oh, and those of you and the two other musketeers, of course. There were no prints on the glass case at all."

"Interesting," I said. "Thanks, Chief. Any other clues that I missed?"

"Unfortunately, no," the chief replied. "As you said, there's nothing much to go on. We're just checking the usual places where a hot item like this might turn up, and keeping in touch with other towns up and down the river as well." I could almost hear his shrug over the phone. "But frankly, I'm not holding out much hope. That thing is probably halfway to the East Coast or Europe or somewhere by now."

"Okay. Thanks again, Chief," I said. "I won't keep you any longer. But if you come up with anything else . . ."

"You'll be the very first noninvolved, non–law-enforcement person I call," the chief said with only a touch of sarcasm in his voice. "Good-bye, Nancy. My best to your father."

"Bye."

I hung up the phone and stood there for a moment, thinking about what I'd just learned. No fingerprints. Did that mean the inside-job theory was right? Or did it just mean that the thief had been careful enough not to leave prints? I'd heard that some wealthy collectors become obsessed with certain items to the exclusion of all else. What if someone like that had heard about Simone's Fabergé egg—a family heirloom that she would surely never agree to sell—and became determined to get it by any means necessary? Such a person would probably hire a professional thief to sneak in and take the egg and *only* the egg. Nothing else in the house would have been of interest.

I shook my head. That whole theory seemed pretty far-fetched. In all my years of observing Dad's cases and solving a few of my own, I've learned that the most obvious solution is usually the right one.

But what was the most obvious solution here? I wasn't sure. There seemed to be two primary possibilities. The first was that someone had happened upon the unlocked house, spotted the egg, grabbed it, and been scared off before having the chance to take anything else. The second was that one of the people in the house—Simone, her nephew, or one of his friends—had taken the egg.

Going to that party later might tell me a lot about the second possibility, I told myself, checking my watch again. But in the meantime, maybe I'd follow up on the first possibility by talking to some more of Simone's neighbors. I could even use the zucchini case as an excuse to get people talking, and then also find out if they saw or heard anything about Simone's case.

I was still staring at the phone when it rang, startling me out of my thoughts. Stepping forward, I grabbed the receiver.

"Hello," I said.

"Nancy!" Bess's familiar voice cried into my ear. "I have some terrible news!"

7

Gathering Clues

My heart raced at the panic in Bess's voice. "What is it?" I exclaimed. "What's wrong, Bess? Tell me! Is someone hurt?"

"Oh, no, nothing like that!" Bess replied, sounding a bit sheepish. "Er, sorry for sounding so upset. But my mother just asked if I could stay with Maggie for a couple of hours—poor kid has an awful stomach virus—which means I probably won't be able to come over and help you pick out an outfit and get ready for the party."

Slowly my heart rate returned to normal. To Bess, there's no emergency quite like a fashion emergency. "I think I'll be able to manage," I told Bess. "And I'll try not to embarrass you."

Bess giggled. "Sorry again for scaring you," she said. "So what are you up to this afternoon?"

I gave her the short version of my thoughts on Simone's case. "So I might go out and talk to more of the neighbors," I continued. "That way I can see if anyone knows anything about the missing egg at the same time that I'm looking for clues about the identity of the zucchini smasher."

Bess and I chatted about the case for a few more minutes. Then her mother called for her, and she had to go.

As I hung up the phone I couldn't help being slightly relieved that Bess wouldn't be coming by to play fashion consultant. It would give me more time to continue my investigations.

Over the next few hours I visited half a dozen houses on Bluff Street. I heard all about Mr. Carr's kidney stones, saw some home movies the Newbergs had taken on their recent trip to Las Vegas, and got to admire the Winters' new wall-to-wall carpeting. But unfortunately I learned nothing of use in my cases except that several other zucchini patches had been vandalized over the past few days. Back home again, I was thinking about that as I stepped into the shower to get ready for the party.

Why would someone want to stomp *only* the

zucchini? I wondered as I adjusted the water. Why not the tomatoes, or the string beans, or the onions? Why just the zucchini?

Thinking about that reminded me of the other case. Why would someone come into Simone's home and steal *only* that Fabergé egg? I realized it was probably the most valuable single object in the house, but there were other items that would certainly be well worth taking. A professional thief, or a paid amateur, wouldn't have passed those other things by, I thought. Even if someone like that had come for the egg, he or she would've at least slipped those jeweled bracelets into a pocket, or grabbed one of the smaller oil paintings or another couple of knick-knacks.

I thought briefly again of my theory about the obsessive art collector. But it didn't seem any more plausible than it had earlier.

Realizing that I was standing absentmindedly beneath the streaming shower jets, I switched off the water, hoping as an afterthought that I'd actually remembered to shampoo my hair. Stepping out of the shower, I toweled off and slipped on my favorite terrycloth robe and fuzzy pink slippers.

As I wandered into my cheerful, yellow-and-white wallpapered bedroom, my mind wandered back to the mystery of the missing egg. I was becoming more and more certain that this case wasn't an ordinary robbery. The more I thought about it, the more likely it seemed that someone in the house must have taken the heirloom. Any other theory meant leaving too much to chance.

But even if I went with that assumption, a couple of big questions remained: Which of the people in the house had taken the egg? And why?

I knew I might be able to find out the answer to both questions that evening at the party, which was now about an hour away. But I wanted to be prepared. Sitting down at my desk, I turned on my computer. It was time to do a little research.

Fifty minutes later I had found out everything I ever needed to know about Fabergé eggs. I read about how Alexander III, then czar of Russia, had commissioned the first one as an Easter gift for his wife, Czarina Maria, and about how Alexander's son—Czar Nicholas II—had continued the tradition upon his father's death, presenting a new egg each year to his mother and one to his wife. Well-known jeweler Peter Carl Fabergé had worked hard every season to outdo himself, creating uniquely beautiful and intricate eggs out of gold, silver, and precious and semiprecious stones, using colorful enameling techniques. The Russian Revolution and the tragic end of the Romanov royal family had ended the imperial egg tradition forever. Fifty-six had been made, and the whereabouts of only forty-four of them was known today.

As I was examining a Web site showing photographs of several of the imperial eggs, I happened to notice the time at the lower right corner of the computer screen. I suddenly realized that Ned would be arriving to pick me up in about ten minutes.

"Yikes," I said, quickly shutting down the computer.

I was suddenly a strawberry-blond version of the Tasmanian devil, whirling around the room pulling myself together. I shuffled through my closet until I found a blouse and skirt Bess had helped me pick out on our last shopping trip. The skirt was a little tight, but it looked okay—and besides, I didn't want to waste time digging up another outfit.

Next I hurried back into the bathroom. My shoulder-length hair was almost dry, and a few minutes with the blow dryer and a brush had it looking pretty good. I was just dabbing on a little eyeshadow when I heard a car pull up outside. Hurrying to the window, and almost tripping myself in my attempt to run in my snug skirt, I saw Ned's car idling at the curb.

As Ned himself climbed out of the driver's seat, I leaned out the open window. "Hang on, I'm coming!" I yelled.

He glanced up at me and gave me a thumbs-up. Once again I briefly considered changing my skirt, but decided it would take too long. Instead, I forced myself to walk at a conservative pace as I grabbed my purse and headed out of my room and down the stairs.

Outside I found Ned waiting for me on the sidewalk. "Okay, I'm ready," I said breathlessly. Now that I had the hang of walking in that tight, straight skirt, I was able to pick up a little speed as I hurried toward him. "Let's go. Do you want to drive or walk?"

Ned glanced at the lower half of my body. At first I thought he was just surprised to see me in a skirt. I couldn't remember the last time I'd worn one, and I imagined he couldn't either. Then he pointed at my feet. "If you're going to wear those, I think we'd better drive," he said.

"Huh?" I looked down. I was still wearing my fuzzy pink bedroom slippers!

"Oops," I said, blushing furiously as Ned laughed. "Guess I'd better change."

"Oh, I don't know," Ned said with another chuckle. "You could start a new fashion trend with those. The sleepy look."

I gave him a playful shove. "Very funny," I said. "And don't you dare tell Bess about this!"

A few minutes later I was wearing shoes, and Ned was parking his car along the curb in front of

Simone's house. Just as we climbed out, we spotted Bess's car coming our way. We waited for Bess and George to park, then the four of us headed for the front door together.

When Simone answered the door, she was wearing a bright smile and a stylish silk skirt. "Hello!" she exclaimed, seeming delighted to see us. "Nancy, George, Bess, I'm so glad to see you all again. And this must be Nancy's boyfriend!" She smiled at Ned.

"Ned Nickerson," Ned introduced himself, holding out his hand. "Thanks for inviting me."

"Thanks for coming, Ned," Simone replied graciously, shaking his hand. "I'm Simone Valinkofsky. Any friend of Nancy's is a friend of mine. I'm sure she's told you I had a bit of a shock here yesterday, and she was enormously comforting."

I'd been planning to wait a little while before broaching the subject of the theft. But since Simone had brought it up, I figured it was okay to jump right in. "Have you heard anything about the egg?" I asked her.

Simone smiled sadly. "Unfortunately, no," she replied. "The police, they say they are looking, but that I should not expect a miracle. I still have hope. . . . Ah, but here I am leaving you standing on the doorstep! Come in, come in. The boys are waiting for us inside."

Pierre and his three friends were in the living

room, which had been transformed into a perfect party spot by flickering candles and plates of tasty food. French music was playing on the stereo, and Thèo was dancing playfully in front of the fireplace like some kind of hula girl. René and Pierre were watching him, laughing as they popped potato chips into their mouths. Only Jacques seemed unamused. He was sitting in a leather armchair in the far corner of the room, staring morosely into space. A glass of soda sat on a table beside him, apparently untouched.

As soon as they noticed our arrival, all four guys—even Jacques—hurried over to say hello. Simone introduced Ned, and the guys greeted him politely, though all of them seemed much more interested in greeting Bess. I had to admit, she looked particularly stunning that night. She was wearing a pale blue dress that flattered her nice figure and peaches-and-cream skin coloring. Soon she was the center of a throng of admirers.

As Ned chatted with Simone, admiring her home, George and I walked over to help ourselves to sodas. "Simone seems pretty cheery for a recent crime victim," George commented in a low voice.

I nodded, having noticed the same thing. "I wonder if she's just putting on a brave front because she's the hostess?" I said. "She probably doesn't want to mope around and make us all feel bad."

George shrugged. "Maybe," she said. "Or maybe she's not all that upset now that she's realized she'll be getting a hefty insurance payment. That should pay for a lot of her moving expenses."

"Maybe," I replied, grabbing a handful of mixed nuts from a silver-plated bowl. "But we don't even know for sure that the egg was insured. I guess I'd better try to find out."

I turned and started back toward Simone and Ned, almost tripping again in my tight skirt. Ned saw my close call, and I could tell he was hiding a smile. If Simone had noticed too, she didn't let on.

"I hope you're enjoying yourself so far, Nancy," she told me sincerely as Ned excused himself to get a drink. "I meant what I said before; you were such a comfort to me yesterday after the theft."

"Thank you, but it was no trouble at all," I assured her. "I wanted to ask you something else about that, if you don't mind."

"Please, ask me anything," she answered immediately. "At this point, you seem to be my only hope of recovering my beloved heirloom. The police think that it has disappeared forever—'gone without a trace,' as they put it."

I stepped to one side and set my soda down on a small table. But I wasn't really trying to get rid of the drink—I wanted to position myself a little better to see if Simone's expression changed when I asked her the next question.

"I know that an heirloom like yours could never really be replaced," I said. "But I was just wondering if you had any special insurance to cover such a valuable item."

Simone looked a bit surprised by the question, but I could see no trace of any other reaction. "It's funny you should ask," she said. "The egg was insured back in France, of course. But the policy ran out just before I moved. I was planning to have it reinsured here by an American company. In fact, I had an appointment with the appraiser on Monday afternoon." She shrugged, a distressed expression playing over her face. "I suppose I will have to cancel that appointment now."

I patted her arm. "I'm sorry I brought it up," I said. "I didn't mean to upset you."

"Don't be silly, Nancy." She smiled bravely. "*You* didn't upset me. Only the thief did that."

At that moment Pierre hurried over, wanting Simone's help with something in the oven, and I stepped away to treat myself to one of the zucchini fritters I'd just noticed on a table nearby. I guessed that they were from Susie Lin's restaurant. Sure enough, the one I sampled tasted just as delicious as all of Susie's other food.

How could anyone smash zucchini when it can be made into food like this? I wondered, my mind wandering briefly back to my other case as I discreetly licked a crumb of fried batter off my fingers.

Glancing around the room, I saw that one of the French guys, René, had convinced Bess to dance with him. They had cleared a space near the fireplace and were both laughing helplessly as they performed some sort of swing dance that seemed to have little to do with the song that was playing at the moment. Meanwhile Pierre had emerged from the kitchen and was chatting with Ned and George, while Thèo was sifting through the pile of CDs near the stereo.

Okay, since everyone else is occupied, I guess I should talk to Jacques first, I thought to myself. Just one problem—where *is* Jacques?

I looked around again, but the tall, slim young man was nowhere to be seen. With a shrug, I walked over to Thèo instead.

"Hi," I said. "Are you enjoying your visit to River Heights so far?"

Thèo looked at me. Up close, I couldn't help noticing how intelligent his brown eyes were. "Very much, *Mademoiselle* Nancy," he said in his heavy French accent. "It is a most charming town, with charming people. All except for one, that is: the one who has taken our dear Simone's lovely egg."

"Yes, it's too bad," I said, keeping my voice as casual as possible. "Such a beautiful family heirloom—it's hard to imagine who could steal such a thing."

"Not so hard," Thèo replied with a shrug. "It is a very valuable art object, one that many might covet. Even back in Paris, I always wondered why Simone did not take more care in safeguarding it."

"I suppose a lot of people feel that their homes are safe, even when they're not," I commented. "A lot of criminals count on that very thing."

"Too true, too true," Thèo said. "Ah, but enough of this sad topic." Pushing aside the pile of CDs, he leaped to his feet and offered me his hand. "Would you do me the honor of dancing with me, lovely Nancy? I am sure your beau would not mind just one dance, would he?"

I blushed slightly. While I'm not exactly a wall-flower, I'm also not accustomed to charming, hand-some Frenchmen showering me with compliments. "I suppose he wouldn't mind," I agreed, taking his hand.

We joined René and Bess on the tiny "dance floor," and soon Pierre and George joined us. Thèo was an excellent dancer, and he had switched the music from the French tunes to one of my favorite CDs. Ned watched for a few minutes, tapping his foot to the music and smiling. When the song changed, he stepped out and tapped Thèo on the shoulder.

"Excuse me, could I cut in?" he said.

Thèo bowed, feigning a look of great disappointment. "Ah, I knew the magic moment was too good to last," he said, placing my hand in Ned's.

I giggled, feeling decidedly popular. But as Ned and I danced together, I found my mind returning to the case. I had to remember that this party wasn't just about having a good time. I had work to do.

When Simone came out of the kitchen with a tray full of hot pastries fresh from the oven, the dancing broke up and everyone rushed to sample the delicious-smelling treats. As I blew on mine to cool it, I found myself standing with Simone's nephew near the fireplace.

I noticed that Pierre was looking at the empty glass case that had once held the Fabergé egg. Someone had closed the door, but otherwise it looked the same as it had the previous evening.

"I wonder if the police have turned up any new leads in your case," I commented casually.

Pierre glanced at me. "I am not holding my breath," he said. "The police who came here, they seemed very pessimistic. I don't think they hold out much hope of finding the egg."

"Yes, well, I'm just so sorry that the theft had to

ruin the good mood surrounding Simone's move here," I said. "And it's also unfortunate that it had to happen so soon after your friends came to town. It's a weird coincidence, isn't it?"

Pierre frowned. "What are you trying to say, Nancy?" he demanded, his voice rising with sudden anger. As he spoke, the song playing on the stereo ended, allowing his words to leap out into the temporary silence. "Are you accusing my friends of something? After all, one could also point out that you and your friends were the only ones in River Heights who knew that the egg was here. What is to stop us from thinking that one of *you* stole it?"

8

The Shadowy Figure

Simone gasped. **"Pierre!" she** cried. "How dare you speak of our guests that way? Nancy and her friends are our only friends here in town. How can you accuse them of such a thing?"

"I'm sorry," Pierre said immediately, looking crestfallen. He clasped his hands in front of him. "Please, Nancy—all of you—please accept my apology. I spoke without thinking, and was only trying to defend my friends."

Everyone else in the room looked decidedly uncomfortable. "What a way to bring down a party, *mon ami*," René said to Pierre, his tone only half joking.

Pierre shook his head. "Really, I spoke without thinking," he said, taking my hand and looking at me earnestly. "I do that sometimes. Nancy, please say that you will forgive me?"

"Of course," I told him. "I don't blame you for defending your friends. I would do the same. And I really didn't mean to accuse them of anything."

I felt like kicking myself. So much for my under-cover investigation; I had just blown any chance of being subtle as I questioned the French guys. I would have to be more careful from now on. If the thief was indeed in the room with me at that very moment, I was sure that he would be much more wary of me now.

As Pierre turned away to apologize to Bess and George, I noticed that Jacques had reappeared from wherever he'd been hiding earlier. He was watching the proceedings with a curious expression on his face—sort of a cross between confusion and indiges-tion.

"Are we all friends again now?" Pierre asked the room at large, interrupting my thoughts. "Please say that we are, or I will never forgive myself."

"Don't be silly." Bess stepped forward and put a hand on his arm, giving him her most flirtatious smile. "Now stop apologizing and dance with me, all right? Because if you don't, René will insist, and my feet just can't take that anymore."

René roared with laughter, Pierre joined in, and within seconds the party was back in full swing. I let out a sigh of relief.

Ned stepped over to join me. "That was interesting," he whispered in my ear. "Do you think it was a guilty conscience speaking?"

"I don't know," I said. "It could be. Or it could have been a quick-tempered but loyal friend speaking. I *did* practically accuse his friends of stealing the egg—or at least he could have easily interpreted it that way."

"I suppose so." Ned looked thoughtful. "Still, it was a pretty extreme reaction."

I had to agree with that. "It's definitely something to think about," I said. "Although the more I get to know Pierre, the more I think he's just one of those impulsive, emotional people. After all, he was the one who decided to throw us a party after knowing us for about thirty seconds."

Ned laughed, and gestured toward the kitchen. "I'm thirsty after all that dancing," he added. "I think I'll go grab another soda. Can I get you anything?"

My gaze wandered toward Jacques, who was just disappearing into the front hall. "No thanks," I told Ned. "I think I'll go see what some of the other suspects are up to. Only this time, I'll try not to actually accuse them of anything until I have more evidence."

Ned chuckled and headed for the kitchen while I caught up with Jacques in the hallway near the front door.

"Nancy," he said when he saw me. "Hello. Are you and your boyfriend enjoying the party?"

"Very much," I answered with a smile. "What about you? You're not trying to sneak out on us, are you?"

Jacques laughed, though I couldn't help noticing that he seemed rather nervous. "No, no, no, not at all," he said. "That is, I just stepped out for a moment. To think. Out here where it's quiet."

"What are you thinking about?" It was a nosy question. For all I knew, he could be thinking about world peace, or the weather, or that he'd forgotten to trim his toenails . . . but that little sixth sense was tingling again, and somehow I suspected that Jacques's behavior had something to do with the case.

Jacques blinked in surprise. "What am I thinking about?" he asked. "Er, come out on the porch and I'll tell you. I—I think I need some fresh air."

"Sure." I followed him eagerly as he stepped out the door onto the wide, slightly creaky planks of the front porch.

Once outside, he took several deep breaths of the pleasantly warm evening air. "Ah, that is much better," he said, staring out toward the houses across the street. "What a lovely night."

I had to agree with that. From Simone's porch I could see Mr. Tracey hurrying to finish mowing his lawn before the last rays of the sun faded, and I heard the faint shouts of kids playing in one of the yards farther down the block. Lights blinked on in several windows as soft summer darkness gently settled over the neighborhood.

I waited as patiently as I could, but he didn't seem inclined to continue speaking. "Well then," I said after a moment or two. "What were you going to say just now? Inside, I mean. You promised you'd tell me." I tried to put a little of Bess's teasing, flirtatious tone into the words. It always seemed to work for her, and Jacques seemed so distracted that anything was worth a try.

As he turned toward me, I held my breath. His expression was serious, almost somber. Was he about to confess to the crime?

He hesitated for a long moment. Then his grim face suddenly broke into a bright, cheerful smile that changed his whole appearance. "Oh, you will think it's silly," he said. "But I was thinking about . . . about my new car."

"Your new car?" It wasn't quite what I was expecting to hear. "What do you mean?"

Jacques laughed, wandering down to one end of the porch and leaning on the railing. "You see, I have always had a love for classic American cars," he explained. "So when I came here with my friends, I thought, Why not buy one? It's something I have always wanted. And so I did."

"You bought a car?" I said uncertainly.

He nodded. "It is a lovely car," he said. "Red paint, a silver racing stripe, sporty fins on the back . . . It cost me quite a bit, and of course I will have to pay to have it shipped back to France. But it will all be worth it, I think. It is a dream come true."

"I'm sure it is," I said politely. "The car sounds very nice."

I couldn't help being disappointed. Was this really all Jacques had on his mind? A moment ago I'd been so sure that he was hiding a guilty conscience about the egg. But now it seemed he had only been distracted by his big purchase.

I gazed thoughtfully out over the porch railing, not really seeing Mr. Geffington's darkened house and yard next door. From Simone's porch I had a clear view over the picket fence that separated the two yards. I could see the entire front yard, plus about half of the vegetable garden, behind the house.

Jacques leaned toward me. "Nancy, I hope you will come for a ride with me someday," he said. "I know you will love this car. It really is an American beauty—much like you."

"Thanks," I said absently, my mind more on the case than on his compliment. "And sure, I'd love to go for a ride sometime."

Just because Jacques isn't going to confess to the crime himself, that doesn't mean I need to give up on finding out any information from him, I reminded myself as Jacques chattered on about his car's paint job. He still might know something that could be useful in the investigation.

I was trying to figure out how to broach the subject when I caught the sight of movement out of the corner of my eye. It was coming from Mr. Geffington's backyard. Something was moving back there in the near-darkness.

I was instantly on alert, leaning over the railing for a better look. Was it just an animal wandering through? Or could it be the return of the zucchini smasher?

I had to find out. "Excuse me, Jacques," I said quickly. "I've got to go check something out."

I had my hands on the porch railing and was ready to vault over when I remembered that I was wearing a skirt. Mentally cursing my poor choice of clothing, I turned and hurried back toward the porch steps instead.

"Wait," Jacques called, sounding confused. "Where are you going, Nancy?"

"I'll be back in a second," I called over my shoulder without slowing down.

I moved, carefully but quickly, down Simone's front walk, still upset at myself for wearing the tight skirt. If I had been wearing jeans or other pants, I could have taken the direct route across the yard and over the picket fence.

But it wasn't worth worrying about. With any luck, the intruder—if that's who I had seen—wouldn't hear me coming this way.

"Nancy!" Jacques's voice floated clearly through the night air. "Wait for me! You shouldn't rush into the night alone—it's not safe!"

I winced. So much for the element of surprise.

Vaguely aware of Jacques's pounding footsteps racing after me, I put on a burst of speed. In just a few more yards I would reach the concrete steps leading down into Mr. Geffington's yard. Meanwhile I peered ahead, trying to spot the movement I'd seen.

There! I thought with a thrill of discovery. Right there—back by the garden fence!

I squinted at the shadowy figure. It was hard to make out who or what it might be; it was moving around in the deeper shadows of a little patch of trees in the side yard near the picket fence. But the important thing was that the figure didn't seem aware that it was being watched.

My heart pounding at the thought of catching the vegetable vandal red-handed—or green-clubbed, as the case might be—I put on another burst of speed. Behind me I heard a flurry of footsteps. Jacques seemed to be catching up to me. I just hoped he would keep quiet for another few seconds.

I leaped for the steps down into the yard. There was no handrail, so I forced myself to slow down a little as I took the first step down.

Suddenly I felt my feet fly out from under me. The night sky tipped upside down as I found myself falling. . . .

Then everything went black.

9

Stalking the Truth

I awoke to the sound of gentle beeping.

That's strange, I thought as I lay there with my eyes closed, drifting in a cloud of blissful near-sleep. My alarm clock doesn't usually sound like that . . .

"Nancy?" a familiar voice said from somewhere very nearby. "Nancy, are you awake? I think she's waking up!"

"Ned?" I croaked. "What are you doing—uh, here . . . ?"

My voice trailed off in surprise as I opened my eyes. Instead of the familiar yellow-and-white striped walls and solid wood furniture of my bedroom, I saw institutional green paint, white sheets, and stainless steel. My mind clearing slightly, I realized I was in the hospital.

In a flash I remembered what had happened to land me there. "I was running," I said, my voice hoarse and unfamiliar. I cleared my throat. "The steps—I heard Jacques behind me—then I fell, I guess. . . ." I willed myself to remember more, but everything after that was a haze.

Ned put a hand on mine. "Shh," he said gently. "It's okay. Don't try to remember too much. The doctors say you hit your head pretty hard."

I sighed and relaxed against the comfortable hospital pillow. "I hit my head," I repeated, the truth of that statement impossible to deny as I noted the dull throbbing at my temple. I put my hand up and felt my face. There was a bandage covering much of my forehead. "What happened?" I asked Ned. "How did you find me?"

"Jacques came running back to the party," Ned explained. "He said you'd slipped on some steps and hit your head. We all ran out and found you conked out in Mr. Geffington's front yard. In fact, by the time we got there, half the neighborhood was rushing out to help. Jacques was yelling pretty loudly as he ran to get us."

I grinned, then winced as the throbbing in my head suddenly increased. "That's me," I said hoarsely. "Always making a scene."

"Luckily Mrs. Zucker had her cell phone in her

pocket," Ned continued, squeezing my hand gently. "She called an ambulance. Ms. Thompson was there too—she's a nurse, you know—and so she sort of took over until the ambulance arrived."

"That was nice," I said, feeling decidedly woozy as my head settled down again. "Where are the others now? Did someone call my dad?"

"They would only let one person come along in the ambulance, so I was elected." Ned reached over and gently pushed back a stray strand of my hair. "Bess and George went back to Simone's; I promised to call them as soon as you woke up. And your dad is on the way. He was out having dinner with a client, so I guess it took the nurse a while to track him down."

I closed my eyes, too tired to take in the information as fast as Ned was giving it. But even in my groggy state, something was bugging me about what had happened. My eyes popped open again and I stared up at my boyfriend questioningly.

"Ned," I said, my voice still sounding raspy and strange. "How did it happen? I'm not that clumsy—how could I wipe out like that? Did I trip over something? Or what?" I remembered that stupid skirt I'd been wearing. But that wasn't enough to make me actually fall down the stairs. Was it?

Ned shook his head. "Sorry, Nancy," he said.

"You're the detective, not me. I don't think any of us even looked at the steps. We were too busy worrying about you."

"Oh. Right. Sorry." I sighed, putting a hand to my throbbing head.

Ned smiled. "Don't be silly," he said softly. "You have nothing to be sorry about. You're just lucky Jacques was right there to go for help." He frowned slightly. What were you and Jacques doing over at Mr. Geffington's, anyway?"

"I thought I saw something moving over there," I explained. "I was going to see if it was the zucchini smasher—"

"Nancy!" My father's voice boomed out as he rushed into the room. "There you are. What happened?"

Ned stood up, allowing Dad to sit down beside my bed. I smiled weakly up at him. His handsome face was creased with worry.

"It's okay, Dad," I said. "I'll be all right. We Drews have hard heads, remember?"

Ned and I quickly filled him in on the basics of what had happened. "The doctor says she's going to be fine, sir," Ned continued. "He wants to keep her under observation for a day or so, but he says it's really just a precaution. She should be as good as new in a few days."

"What a relief," Dad said, leaning down to plant a kiss on my forehead. "Now, Nancy, what was that you were saying when I came in? Don't tell me that investigating that silly zucchini thing actually got you hurt?"

"Not really," I assured him quickly, concerned by the alarmed look on his face. The last thing I wanted was for him to get worried enough to insist that I drop the case. "It was just my own clumsiness. I was moving so fast that I guess I tripped over my own feet."

"Hmm." Dad looked only half convinced.

"Anyway," I added, "I haven't had a chance to tell you yet, but I have another case I'm working on as well." Dad had left early that morning for a golf game, so I hadn't had a chance to share the story of Simone's theft with him.

Now I wanted his input. Did anything I'd learned at the party mean anything? I thought about Pierre's extreme reaction to my "accusation" of his friends. Did he know something I didn't know? And what about Jacques's weird behavior a little later. Had I really fallen down those steps all on my own?

But before I could say anything else, a nurse bustled in. "All right, you two," she said briskly. "You can see that she's still alive. And she'll still be here tomorrow, so you can finish catching up then. For now, I'm afraid visiting hours are over."

For a moment I thought Dad was going to argue. He can be pretty convincing when he wants to be; if he wanted to extend the visiting hours, he probably could.

But he just sighed and bent down to kiss me again. "Get some sleep, sweetheart," he told me. "We'll see you tomorrow."

The next morning a nurse brought in my breakfast.

"When do visiting hours start?" I asked as she set the tray on the table beside the bed and started arranging my covers.

"Not for a few hours, I'm afraid, dear," the nurse replied cheerily. "But don't worry, I'm sure your loved ones will be here as soon as they possibly can."

I was disappointed. My head was feeling much clearer and immediately upon waking up I'd started thinking about Simone's case. There were a few things about it that still didn't make much sense, and I really wanted to discuss them with someone.

The nurse picked up the tray and set it in front of me. "Can I make phone calls before then?" I asked her.

"Of course!" The nurse gestured to the phone on the bedside table. "But eat your breakfast first, okay, dear? You need to get your strength back up so you'll be ready to leave tomorrow."

I smiled and took a bite of scrambled egg. But as soon as the nurse left the room, I pushed the tray aside and grabbed the phone.

When George picked up, she sounded very happy to hear from me. "How are you feeling?" she asked. "When are they letting you out of there?"

"Better, and I'm not sure," I replied. "They said probably tomorrow morning sometime. I was hoping it would be today, but the doctor really wants me to stay one more night just in case." I sighed loudly. "That means I'm going to lose another whole day of trying to track down who took that egg. I'm afraid the trail is going to get cold."

"Maybe," George said. "But if you want, Bess and I could try to do a little more investigating for you today."

I hadn't thought of that possibility. "Really?" I said, feeling a little wistful. I still wished I could be out there investigating myself, but having my friends do it seemed like the next best solution. "You guys would do that? That's great! I was really hoping to find out more from Pierre's friends last night. Maybe you guys could talk to them. We don't want them to know we suspect them, though. Not after that little scene with Pierre last night. Do you think you could find an excuse to hang out with them?"

George laughed. "Come on, Nancy," she chided.

"These are *guys* we're talking about. We won't need an excuse as long as Bess is there looking cute and smiling at them."

I giggled. "Good point!"

"Besides, Pierre already called me this morning to see when we could stop by again," George added. "Guess what: He and the other guys are pooling their money to send you a big bunch of flowers. They picked it up this morning."

"How sweet!" I said.

George laughed. "It is—but you might not say that if you'd heard them arguing over the price last night after you left for the hospital," she said. "Poor Jacques just about fainted when he heard how much it was going to cost for the kind of bouquet the others wanted to get you. I guess he doesn't have much money. In fact, René told Bess that he and Thèo had to chip in on Jacques's plane ticket to the U.S."

"Really?" I poked at my scrambled egg as I recalled my conversation with Jacques the previous evening. "Then how did he afford the car he just bought?"

"Car?" George said. "What are you talking about?"

I told her what Jacques had said about his new purchase. "He made it sound like he'd just bought it," I added. "Like, he paid in cash right away or something. I didn't really ask too much about it, because I didn't think it was important at the time."

"It's probably not." George sounded disinterested. "Maybe he was just showing off. Bess said she thought he had a little crush on you."

"Really?" I blushed, wondering if that was true. I'm pretty observant about most things, but I don't always notice when a guy shows interest in me *that* way. Call it a blind spot. "Well, never mind that. It's still sort of weird—about the car, I mean." I filed away the question about Jacques's financial status for future thought. "I guess you should put extra effort into finding out more about Jacques."

"Definitely," George said. "We all think it's a little strange how you happened to fall down those stairs, Nancy. That's not like you."

"I know." I popped a grape from the breakfast tray into my mouth. "But I *was* wearing that funny skirt. I could hardly walk in it, let alone run down those steps."

I could almost hear George shaking her head skeptically. "I'm not buying it," she said. "You hit your head pretty hard. That wouldn't have happened if you had just tripped. Even without a handrail, you still would've caught yourself with your hands or something. You might have ended up with a broken wrist, but not a concussion."

"So what are you saying?"

"I'm saying the fall couldn't have been that simple," George replied. "There had to be something weird about it. I mean, you were tripped or pushed or something."

"Are you saying you think Jacques shoved me down the steps?" I had to admit, it wasn't the first time the thought had occurred to me. Just how close behind me had those rushing footsteps been? I tried to think back, to relive the moment, but I just wasn't sure. The entire memory was still a little fuzzy. I didn't remember feeling a shove, but I didn't remember hitting my head, either, and obviously *that* had happened.

"What else could it have been?" George replied to my question. "I mean, you two disappear outside, and five minutes later he comes rushing in saying you slipped and knocked yourself out."

"How did he describe the fall, anyway?" I asked curiously, shifting the phone to my other ear and wincing as it grazed my injured temple. "Did he offer any explanation for it?"

"Not really. He just said your feet flew out from under you halfway down the steps, you fell backward and sideways, and then hit the side of your head on the stone."

I touched my aching temple. "Well, that last part certainly matches the evidence," I said wryly. "But even if Jacques is lying, why on earth would he want to hurt me?"

"Weren't you questioning him about the disappearance of the egg?" George asked. "Maybe he heard what Pierre said earlier—about you accusing his friends, I mean. Maybe Jacques figured you were getting too close to some answers."

"But I wasn't getting close to any answers at all," I exclaimed.

"If he has a guilty conscience, all that matters is whether he *thought* you were figuring things out."

I had to admit she had a point. "I guess we still can't rule anything—or anyone—out at this point," I said. "I really wish I could be out there with you guys today. If someone in this group does have a guilty conscience, he might be getting antsy, especially after my accident. Maybe the best thing to do, on second thought, is to watch these guys from a *distance* and see if one of them makes a move."

"Bess and I will do what we can," George promised. "After all, we've learned from the best! We'll just go out there and ask ourselves, 'What would Nancy Drew do?' We'll stop by later during visiting hours and let you know how it goes."

I giggled. "Okay," I said. "Good luck. And be careful!"

I spent the rest of the morning reading and watching TV—and trying not to think too much about my cases, since I couldn't do anything about them at the moment anyway. When visiting hours started, Dad and Hannah came by with some new magazines and some of Hannah's fresh-baked cookies. While they were in my room, the bouquet from Pierre and the other guys arrived, along with more flowers from Simone and a few cards from other neighbors.

Eventually Dad and Hannah left, and I found myself waiting impatiently for news from my friends. Had they found out anything important? Were they figuring things out without me?

The seconds seemed to tick by at the speed of glacial melting. For a while I was afraid visiting hours were going to end before my friends got there. But finally I heard Bess's familiar giggle out in the hallway. A second later George appeared in the doorway of my room.

"Sorry we're late," George said. "And Bess might be a few more minutes. She found a cute young medical resident to flirt with out there."

Bess hurried in and gave her cousin a shove. "I wasn't flirting," she insisted, her cheeks flushed so deeply that they almost matched the hot-pink jacket she was wearing. "I was just being polite. What did you want me to do, ignore him when he said hello?"

George rolled her eyes. I laughed and gestured for them both to come closer.

"How are you feeling?" Bess asked me, hurrying over with a look of concern and sitting down carefully on the edge of my bed. "Does your head still hurt?"

"A little, but it's getting better," I said. "But never mind that. Shut the door so we can talk, okay?"

George nodded and turned back toward the door. "She must be feeling okay—she's giving us orders," she quipped.

"So?" I asked as soon as she pulled the door shut. Luckily I had a private room, so we didn't have to worry about being overheard. "Did you have any luck today?"

Bess and George exchanged a glance. "Well, sort of," Bess said at the same time that George said, "Not exactly."

"Tell me," I said, settling back against my pillow.

George sat down in one of the visitor's chairs beside my bed and crossed her legs. "After I talked to you this morning, I called Bess." She hooked a thumb in her cousin's direction. "She was still getting dressed, so I figured I had about two hours to kill—"

"Stop!" Bess protested, shooting her a dirty look. "She's just being silly. I left to pick her up almost right away."

"True," George admitted. "Looking back, I guess I should've given her more time to choose an appropriate wardrobe for a stakeout. But more about that in a minute."

I cast a curious glance at Bess's outfit. In addition to the hot-pink cotton jacket, she was wearing a matching pink-and-white-striped T-shirt, white capri pants, and cute pink sandals. It wasn't exactly an inconspicuous outfit, especially on someone who was already as eye catching as Bess. George was dressed much more discreetly, in jeans and a dark T-shirt.

"Anyway," George went on, "while I was waiting for her to pick me up, I went online to see if I could find out anything interesting about our suspects."

"Great idea!" I said, wishing I'd thought of it earlier. George has been the information systems manager for her mother's catering business since junior high. She spends more time online than anyone I know. If there's something you want on the Web, she's the one to track it down. "So what did you find out?"

"Not much," George admitted. "I barely had time to log on before Bess got to my house. But I'm planning to do more checking when I get home."

"Cool," I said. "So then what did you guys do?"

Bess took over the story. "We drove over to your neighborhood and parked in front of your house, since we figured that would look less suspicious if anyone was paying attention."

"See? We *have* been learning from you!" George interrupted with a grin.

I laughed. "Good plan," I said. "Then what?"

"We walked over toward Simone's house," Bess continued, smoothing out a wrinkle in my bedspread. "We found a good spot behind some shrubs across the street, hid ourselves, and waited."

"Don't forget, first we went and peeked in the window," George reminded her. She glanced at me. "We didn't want to hang around there all day just to find out everyone left early for doughnuts or something. It was my idea to check."

"Right," Bess said, rolling her eyes. "And it was also your idea to stick your big old head up right in the middle of the kitchen window. It's a miracle they didn't see you."

"Well, they didn't," George said, sitting up straighter in the visitor's chair. "Anyway, everyone was still home. After what we talked about this morning, Bess and I decided that if the guys split up when they went out, we were going to follow Jacques."

"He's definitely the most likely suspect after what happened to you, Nancy," Bess agreed.

They looked so pleased with their own decision that I just nodded and smiled. While I agreed that there were certainly some odd things going on with

Jacques, I almost wished they'd decided to follow René or Thèo. I felt as though I'd hardly had a chance to talk with either of them. I would have liked to know a little more about them. What if we were focusing all this attention on the wrong suspect, while the real thief or thieves were dancing around right under our noses?

But I kept quiet as George picked up the story again. "After breakfast Simone drove off somewhere, and Pierre and Thèo went out in the backyard and started hacking at that overgrown garden back there. We watched them for a while, until Jacques came out the front door."

Bess nodded eagerly. "He looked really suspicious, too. He kept checking over his shoulder, like he didn't want to be seen leaving."

"And he headed for town, on foot," George said meaningfully. "No sign of any fancy sports car."

"Interesting," I said. "Did you follow him?"

"Of course!" Bess said. "We stayed back a few blocks until we got downtown, where it was easier to stay close without being seen."

I glanced at Bess's footwear, impressed as always at how she seemed to find strappy, flimsy sandals as comfortable as most people found sneakers. "So where did he go?"

George leaned toward the bedside table to help

herself to one of Hannah's cookies. "He went to a few different places," she said through a mouthful of crumbs. "It turned out to be a little tricky trying to keep track of him without letting him see us."

"Yes," Bess agreed. "You know, in the movies that sort of thing always looks so easy. But it's really not."

My sixth sense was tingling again, but this time it had nothing to do with Jacques, or the case as such. I had a feeling my friends weren't telling me something. "So what are you two saying?" I asked. "Did Jacques catch you following him?"

Bess looked sheepish. "Well, I guess we weren't being quite as sneaky as we thought," she began.

"What's this 'we' stuff?" George broke in with a snort. "I'm not the one who decided to dress up like a neon sign! You could see that pink jacket from outer space."

I was starting to get the picture. "So Jacques saw you?"

"A few times, I guess," Bess admitted. "We had followed him into that big antique store on River Street, and George and I split up to try to stay out of sight more easily. I was sort of sneaking around this big urn thingie when I accidentally took a step too far and ended up face-to-face with Jacques." She shrugged. "He didn't really seem that weirded out or anything. He just asked how you were doing, and

105

then mentioned that he thought he'd seen me in Olde River Jewelers. So he asked if I was following him."

"He was joking," George put in. "Obviously. But Miss Supersleuth here panicked."

"Maybe a little." Bess blushed. "I—um—I sort of told him I *was* following him, but only because I was feeling too shy to just walk up and say hello. Because, you know, I thought he was so cute at the party and all. . . ."

"Yikes," I said with a grin. "So did he buy it?"

Bess smiled modestly. "He seemed to. I think he was about to ask me out, actually. But then George popped out from behind a pile of old Oriental rugs—"

"Hey, I thought you were about to blow our whole cover!" George exclaimed. "So I, you know, came to the rescue. At that point, I guess Jacques thought we were a little weird."

"Just a little?" I teased. My friends' whole day was starting to sound like an old Keystone Kops routine.

"Anyway, George decided to distract him by giving him the third degree," Bess said.

George shrugged. "Hey, the best defense is a good offense, right?" she said. "So I just asked him why he was wandering around town on foot if he's got this fancy new car he's been bragging about. That threw him for a loop."

"Yeah, he sort of turned red and then mumbled something about it being in the shop," Bess said. "That seemed sort of weird. I mean, a brand-new car already in the shop? So naturally, I asked him what was wrong with it."

I wasn't surprised. Bess loves cars like George loves computers. She fixed up her own car herself, and can diagnose a damaged gasket or a blown engine from a mile away.

"So, he was totally tongue-tied!" Bess continued, throwing up her hands in remembered amazement. "He doesn't know what's wrong with it? Come on! So I mention a few possibilities, and he's still totally clueless. He doesn't even know if the car's got an overhead cam. But what guy in his right mind wouldn't know something like that about his brand-new sports car?"

Even though I had no idea what an overhead cam was myself, I had to admit she had a point. I'm a total dunce about cars, but Jacques's story was starting to sound more and more suspicious.

"He really did look pretty uncomfortable," George added. "He obviously had no idea how to answer any of Bess's questions about the car. He eventually made some lame excuse and took off."

Bess smiled. "We decided not to follow him back to Simone's, though, for obvious reasons."

"Interesting," I said, musing on what my friends had just reported. "Now tell me all the stores he went into while you were following him."

"Oh! Right. That's important," George said. "He went to a jewelry store, a secondhand consignment-type store, and three antique stores." She ticked them off on her fingers, then paused to let the information sink in. "But he didn't buy anything."

10

Connections and
Opportunities

I was still thinking about Jacques's "errands" when visiting hours ended and a nurse arrived to shoo my friends out of the room. A jewelry store, a consignment shop, and antique stores. All of those places seemed likely choices to hock a stolen egg. I had to admit, Jacques was starting to look more and more like our top suspect.

But it wasn't as if Jacques had actually pulled out the egg at any of the shops. Was he just scoping the best place to unload it for some quick cash? Or were we still missing something, some important piece of the puzzle? I was still thinking about it through dinner and as I drifted off to sleep.

. . . .

When I woke up the next morning, my head felt much better. My mind jumped straight back to my cases. I couldn't wait to get out of the hospital and get back to work on them.

I was just finishing breakfast when the phone rang. It was Simone calling to see how I was doing.

"I'm feeling much better," I assured her, pushing away my tray. "They're supposed to let me out of here sometime this morning."

"Oh, that is wonderful!" Simone sounded relieved. "We've been so worried about you, Nancy. I feel so terrible about your fall. I feel that it was partially my fault because it happened at my party."

"Don't feel that way," I told her. "It was just an accident. The only thing to blame is my own clumsiness."

"Pierre keeps telling me the same thing." Simone laughed. "Oh, not about your clumsiness of course," she added quickly. "But that it must have been an accident, just as Jacques told us." She sighed. "I've been so glad to have Pierre here through all of this. It has been a great comfort having someone familiar stay with me in this new place. Who knew that he and I could end up so close, being the children of two such jealous, warring fathers? But after all that's happened, Pierre feels more like my brother than my nephew. Oh! Here he is—he must have heard his name. Just a moment, please, Nancy."

I waited, leaning back against my pillow and staring at the greenish beige walls. I couldn't help wondering what that comment of Simone's meant. It definitely sounded as if her father and Pierre's father didn't get along. Was there a story there? It would have been pushy of me to ask for more information, but I was curious. It might not have any bearing on the case of the missing egg, but then again, it never pays to ignore a possible clue, no matter how unlikely it might seem at first.

As I tried to think of a polite way to find out more, Simone came back on the line. "Nancy, Pierre is eager to speak with you," she said. "I'll put him on now."

"Okay," I said.

"Nancy!" Pierre's voice cried into my ear a second later. "You're still alive!"

I chuckled. "Yep, that's what they tell me," I said. "I hope I didn't scare you all too much."

"Oh, you gave us quite a fright," Pierre replied. "Seeing you lying there, so still . . . Well, it put things in perspective."

"What do you mean?" I asked.

Pierre sighed. "Oh, Nancy," he said sorrowfully. "Simone has told me that you want to help her get her egg back. But we both agree that no heirloom, no matter how valuable, is worth getting hurt over. If someone pushed you down those steps . . ." His voice trailed off.

I didn't bother to point out to him that I'd actually been working on the zucchini case at the time of my accident. I was touched by the worry in his voice.

"I appreciate your concern," I told him. "But nobody is saying for sure that I was pushed. I probably just tripped and fell." I still wasn't one hundred percent sure about that. But until I got some evidence to the contrary, it seemed the most likely scenario. Hadn't I almost tripped myself in that skirt several times earlier?

"Hmm." Pierre didn't sound convinced. "Well, yes, that's what Jacques told us happened. . . ." His voice faded again for a moment. "Anyway," he went on, "it's starting to seem like a job for the police. I don't want to see you hurt again, and neither does Simone. It would simply destroy us if that happened."

"You don't have to worry about me," I said. "And I'm sure the River Heights police will find that egg soon."

I wasn't sure about any such thing. And I certainly wasn't planning on giving up on the case. But I didn't want to worry Pierre and Simone by telling them that right now. Once I was out of the hospital, I could figure out how to proceed. I said good-bye to the pair and hung up.

Just as the handset hit the cradle, the phone rang again. This time George was on the other end of the line.

"So are they springing you today or what?" she demanded immediately.

I grinned. "I sure hope so!" I said. "I'm ready to get out of here. Did you find out anything more since yesterday?"

"As a matter of fact, I did," George said. "Hold on a sec. Bess is here with me, and she's poking me in the arm and making faces. I think she wants to talk to you too."

A second later I heard another extension pick up. "Nancy?" Bess said breathlessly. "Are you there? How are you feeling?"

I assured her that I was still in one piece. "Anyway," I said, "George, what were you saying? You found out more about the case?"

"Sort of," George said. "I did a little snooping on-line last night. Namely, I found out that there's no car registered in Jacques's name. Not in France, and not here. Zippo. Nada. Which means that if he really does have some fancy sports car, he didn't get it legally."

"Well, we don't know for sure that it even exists," I pointed out, smiling at the nurse who had just entered to retrieve my breakfast tray. I waited a second until she had bustled out of the room, then added,

"He could just be making up the whole story for some reason."

"Or maybe he just hasn't registered it yet," Bess said. "He did say he just bought it, right?"

"True," I said as the nurse returned, along with my father. "Oops," I told my friends. "I have to go. I think they're finally releasing me. I'll call you when I get home."

An hour later my dad pulled his car to the curb in front of our house. "Are you sure you're feeling all right?" he asked me. "I can cancel my meetings and stay home with you if you like."

I rolled my eyes and smiled. He'd asked me the same question at least a dozen times already on the fifteen-minute drive from the hospital. "I'm fine, Dad," I told him patiently. "Even the doctor said I'm good as new, remember? I appreciate the ride home, but you can definitely go on to the office now."

"Well, okay," he said with a slightly sheepish smile. "But I want you to get some rest this afternoon, okay? Just let Hannah take care of you."

At that moment Hannah herself appeared in the doorway and hurried out to meet us. I let her help me out of the car and up the front walk into the house, even though I really did feel fine.

Soon I was tucked into bed with Hannah bustling

114

around, waiting on me hand and foot. She brought me magazines to read, then made me lunch. After she'd taken my tray away and had loaded the dishwasher, she stuck her head into my room.

"Nancy, I'm just going to step out to run some errands," she told me. "Will you be all right here by yourself until I get back?"

"Of course," I assured her. "Don't worry about me. Take your time."

As soon as I heard her car start up and pull away, I hopped out of bed. I'd done enough resting for one day. I was itching to get back on the case.

I was pulling on some clothes when the phone rang. I grabbed it, guessing that it was my father calling to check on me.

"Hello?" a soft, accented voice said. "Is *Mademoiselle* Nancy at home, please?"

"This is Nancy," I said, immediately recognizing the voice. "Is this Jacques?"

"Yes, it is I," Jacques replied, sounding a little shy. "I—I just wanted to call and inquire how you are feeling. Pierre told me you were coming out of the hospital today."

"That's right," I said, leaning against my dresser and propping the phone on my shoulder so I could run a comb through my hair. "And I'm feeling fine, thanks."

"Oh, that is good news." Jacques sounded relieved. "I still keep thinking that if only I had been a little closer, I might have been able to catch you. I am sorry to say that I did not even see that you were falling until your head hit the steps."

"Really?" I dropped the comb and stood up straight, suddenly very interested. "I thought the others said you saw me trip and fall."

Jacques hesitated. "Not exactly," he said. "That is, I saw it out of the corner of my eye—enough to see that your feet went forward and your head went back. But at the time you started down the steps, my attention was distracted by something else."

I pressed the phone to my ear. "What?" I asked, instantly remembering that shadowy shape in Mr. Geffington's yard. "Did you see something?"

"I—I think so," he said hesitantly. "I spotted a figure running through the bushes in the yard we were entering. I turned to see what it was. When I turned back, you were falling."

"Did you get a look at the figure?" I asked. "Was it a person? How tall?"

"I'm sorry," he replied. "I did not see it very well. It might have been a person crouching down, but it also might have been an animal, perhaps a large dog? I only caught a glimpse before I heard you call out and turned to see you hit the ground."

After I finished assuring him again that I was fine, we said our good-byes and hung up. I stared at the phone for a moment, thinking about the conversation. Why had Jacques called? Was it really just to check on me, or was he trying to determine how much I remembered? I wasn't sure. He'd sounded genuinely worried about me, and hadn't really questioned me about my memory of the accident. Did that mean something?

I shook my head with frustration. So far the only clues I had seemed to point to Jacques as the most likely culprit. His loner behavior at the party. The wild story about the sports car that might or might not really exist. His presence at the scene of my mysterious accident. His odd "errands" when Bess and George followed him.

But even given all that, I just couldn't make the Jacques-as-thief theory add up in my head. The trouble was, I wasn't having much luck coming up with alternative ideas. All I knew was that *someone* had taken the egg, and that someone obviously didn't want to be caught.

I picked up the phone to call Bess and George.

My friends arrived a few minutes later. I'd tried to call Ned, too, but he was out somewhere with his father.

"So?" George said as she and Bess entered the

house. "Now that you're on the loose again, have you wrapped up your cases yet?"

"Not exactly," I admitted. I perched on the edge of the antique bench in the front hallway, still feeling a little weak from my two days in bed. My head was also a little achy. But my mind was feeling as strong as ever, and I'd spent my time waiting for my friends by thinking again about the egg case. "Actually, I wanted to ask you more about the day you followed Jacques," I told my friends. "How did he seem while he was going into those stores? You know—his mood, his expression. That kind of thing." I still had the feeling there was something I was missing, and I wouldn't rest until I figured it out. After all, it could be the key to cracking the whole case.

George's eyes lit up. "Aha!" she said. "So you're starting to believe he's guilty?"

I shook my head. "No, I'm starting to believe he might be the only one who's definitely *not* guilty."

"Really?" Bess sounded surprised. "But all the clues point to him."

"I know," I told them both. "And that's why I think someone might be trying to frame him for the theft. And for my accident."

"Is this another one of your hunches?" George asked skeptically.

I shrugged. "Maybe," I said. "But I also just don't

think the clues really add up. I mean, Jacques's obviously not a stupid guy. Why would he push me down those steps when he knew he'd be setting himself up to look guilty? And if he wanted to sell stolen property, would he really wander around town in broad daylight? In fact, would he be dumb enough to try to hock the Fabergé egg right here in River Heights?"

"Hmm. I guess that's a good point." Bess looked thoughtful. "Come to think of it, he didn't even seem that nervous when we were following him—not until he saw George and me, at least."

George frowned. "He did seem a little weird, though," she told Bess. "Remember? You commented on his expression. It looked like he was angry or worried or something."

"Right," Bess agreed. "But not nervous, exactly. Not like someone with valuable stolen property in his backpack."

"But what about that weird car story?" George asked, leaning against the wall. "What's up with that?"

I shrugged. "That part still doesn't make sense to me, either," I said. "I mean, if we'd actually seen some expensive sports car, it would definitely be a big clue since we know he doesn't have much money. But there's no car to be seen, and no registration, either."

Bess nodded sadly. "Too bad," she murmured. "That car sounded pretty cool."

"Well, I'm still not totally convinced," George said. "But I guess it wouldn't hurt to check out some other leads. So what do you have in mind, Nancy?"

"I want to go over to Simone's," I said. "I've hardly had a chance to talk to René or Thèo. And I'm a little worried about Jacques. If someone really is trying to frame him for this, he could be in danger. Especially if that someone had anything to do with my fall."

"What do you mean?" Bess asked, looking concerned.

I thought back to my last conversation with Jacques. "There was a shadowy figure in Mr. Geffington's yard," I told my friends. "That's why I ran over there; I thought it might be the zucchini smasher. Jacques mentioned that he saw it too. But what if that figure had something to do with the stolen egg? Did anyone else leave the room between the time I went outside to talk to Jacques and when he came back to the house after I fell?"

"I don't know," George said. "I was in the bathroom around that time, and then on the way back I stopped to read this framed family history thing hanging in the hall."

"I'm not sure either," Bess said. "The only one I can vouch for is Simone. I think that was around the time I was helping her slice some brownies in the kitchen."

I made a mental note of Simone's probable alibi.

Then I bit my lip, wishing I could get ahold of Ned. He would probably be able to tell me if any of the other French guys had left the room at any point. But I didn't want to wait around until he got home. Now that I'd realized that someone could be out to frame Jacques, I was worried about him.

"I think we'd better get over to Simone's pronto," I said. "I want to talk to Jacques first. And then, if I can, I want to get some more information out of the other guys."

Bess looked worried. "Are you sure you feel up to it?" she asked. "You still look a little pale."

"I'm fine," I said. "It's just a short walk, and I could use the fresh air."

Bess and George both seemed convinced by that. I tried not to think about what Hannah or my father would say if they were there.

We headed outside. Soon we were approaching Simone's house. As we passed Mr. Geffington's yard, I glanced curiously toward the bushes in the backyard where I'd seen that figure. They were thick, but not very tall—perhaps four feet at the most. Could one of the French guys have stooped down enough to run through the bushes without his head sticking up over the top? It would be awfully awkward, I decided.

I was about to ask George to go down there and

try it herself, just to see how it would look. But just then Bess let out a gasp and pointed ahead.

"Look," she cried. "Up on the ladder. Isn't that Jacques up th—oh, no!"

I spun around and looked to where she was pointing. There was a tall ladder propped against the back of Simone's house—we could see it sticking up past the roofline—and Jacques was clinging to the top rung. I was just in time to see the ladder teeter sideways. It rocked back again, and then swung out of view as it crashed to the ground.

11

Accidents and Answers

My friends and I raced around the house into the backyard. Pierre was there, bending over Jacques's still figure. The ladder lay nearby.

"Call an ambulance!" I shouted, and Bess peeled off toward the house.

"No, you can't get in," Pierre cried when he saw where she was going. "We were locked out. That's why we got out the ladder."

George and I skidded to a stop beside Pierre. "What happened?" George cried, staring down at Jacques. "Is he okay?"

"I don't know," Pierre exclaimed, his voice shaking. "We were working in the yard and accidentally locked ourselves out. We weren't sure when Simone and the others would return, so Jacques offered to climb up to one of the second-story windows. I was still hacking away at the vines by the vegetable patch, and had my back to him as he climbed. I heard him let out a shout, and turned around just in time to see him fall."

Just then Jacques stirred and let out a groan. "It's okay," I told him soothingly, kneeling beside him. "Just lie still, okay? Help will be here soon."

Bess hurried over. "What should we do?" she asked anxiously. "I wish I had my cell phone on me."

"Never mind." I hopped to my feet. "I'll run across the street. Mrs. Zucker works at home during the day. You guys stay here with him, and don't let him move."

Without waiting for an answer, I raced around the side of the house. There was no traffic on the street at that time of day, so I ran across, without stopping, toward the Zuckers' home a few houses down. The other houses on the block all looked quiet and empty. At that hour most people were still at work.

Little Owen Zucker was swinging his baseball bat around in the driveway. "Nancy!" he cried when he saw me. "Want to play?"

I stopped in front of him, panting. The run had taken more out of me than I'd expected. The sore spot on my head was throbbing again. "Sorry, Owen, not right now," I wheezed, bending over and resting my hands on my knees. "Could you run inside and get your mom? Tell her it's an emergency."

Owen's eyes widened. "Okay," he said. "Here, hold this."

He shoved the baseball bat into my hands and took off for the door. I leaned gratefully on the bat, ignoring the gooey handle, and tried to get my breath back as I waited for Mrs. Zucker.

A little less than an hour later, I was sitting on Simone's porch with Bess and George. Pierre had gone along with Jacques in the ambulance, promising to call when he had any news. Bess had even run back to my house to fetch her cell phone from her car so she wouldn't miss the call.

Simone was still out shopping, though René and Thèo had returned a few minutes after the ambulance had departed. After we told them what had happened, they waited with us for a while, but both of them seemed too distracted and worried to sit still. Finally they went back inside to fetch us some cold drinks. While we waited for them to return, my friends and I talked about the case.

"Okay," Bess commented, glancing at her cousin. "I guess this means Nancy was right. Maybe Jacques is being framed."

George shrugged. "Maybe," she said. "Although, if

you think about it, this would be a really great way for a clever thief to throw us off the track."

Bess snorted. "Yeah, right," she said. "By flinging himself off a ladder? Doesn't sound too clever to me."

I smiled slightly at their bickering, but my mind was racing. Bess was right—this was one more piece of the puzzle. But how could I prove Jacques hadn't stolen the egg? More importantly, how could I figure out who *had*?

Drumming my fingers on the arm of my wicker chair, I ignored the slight throb of pain in my head as I tried to think harder. "I just feel like there's something . . . ," I whispered, more to myself than to my friends. "Some clue, some bit of information I'm not remembering—"

"Hey," George interrupted my train of thought. "Look. Here comes Mr. Geffington. Wonder if he heard all the commotion just now."

I glanced up. Sure enough, Mr. Geffington was just coming down Simone's steps from the street.

"Nancy Drew!" he exclaimed, hurrying toward the porch. "I heard you had a bit of an accident out in front of my house the other night. I hope you're all right?"

"I'm fine," I said. "Sorry I haven't been able to focus on your zucchini case."

"I understand, of course. Anyway, I still think it's

Safer behind both incidents. You know how those dramatic types can hold a grudge." He scowled in the direction of his other neighbor's house.

I blinked, realizing what he had just said. "Wait," I insisted. "You said '*both* incidents.' Do you mean something else happened in your garden? Besides the smashing I know about from last Tuesday night?"

"As a matter of fact, yes," Mr. Geffington said. "I planted some new zucchini after the first incident. They were doing nicely, growing fast and starting to form little fruits. But the scoundrel struck again! I had to clean the remains off my front steps on Sunday morning." He clenched his fists angrily. "He must have stomped every plant and wiped his feet on his way out just to taunt me!"

Something clicked into place in my head. "Sunday morning?" I repeated. "You found—uh—zucchini remains on your front steps on Sunday morning? You mean the steps leading up to the sidewalk?"

"Of course," Mr. Geffington replied, sounding a bit testy. "You don't think the zucchini vandal broke into my house and smeared sticky, slimy zucchini all over my staircase, do you?"

Bess giggled, then clapped a hand over her mouth. Meanwhile I was finally putting two and two together. Sticky, slimy zucchini. On those stone steps. If Mr. Geffington had discovered it there on Sunday morning, that meant the vegetable vandal had probably struck again on . . .

"Saturday night," I said aloud. "Just in time to make me slip down those steps."

George heard me and shot me a startled look. "Wait," she said. "Are you saying what I think you're saying?"

I nodded. "Jacques didn't have anything to do with my fall," I said. "Neither did anyone connected with the egg theft. I just slipped on—"

"Zucchini!" all three of us said at once.

Mr. Geffington looked confused. "What?" he demanded. "What are you talking about? Who's Jacques, and what do eggs have to do with this?"

"Well, it's sort of a long story . . . ," I began.

Just then the front door opened and René and Thèo emerged from the house and moved onto the porch. Thèo was carefully carrying a trayful of glasses, while René held a pitcher of what looked like lemonade.

"Any news?" Thèo asked immediately, glancing toward Bess's cell phone.

Bess shook her head. "Not yet," she told the French guys.

I introduced Mr. Geffington, who chatted politely for a moment or two and then excused himself. "If I want to have any zucchini at all this summer, I'd better get back to the garden center," he said, shaking his head sorrowfully before hurrying away.

Thèo looked perplexed. "What was that about?" he asked. "Zucchini—is that not a sort of vegetable?"

I was about to try to explain when a shrill, beeping version of the theme from *Star Wars* began to play. Bess shot George a dirty look and grabbed her cell phone from the porch railing. "Let me guess," she said. "You've been reprogramming my ringer again."

George grinned mischievously. "Just answer the phone," she told her cousin.

Bess said hello, then listened for a moment. The rest of us waited eagerly. I could hear the tinny mumble of the voice on the other end. It sounded like Pierre—and it sounded like he was very excited. But I couldn't tell if he was excited in a good way or a bad way. I held my breath.

Finally Bess's pretty face broke into a wide smile. "Oh, that's such a relief!" she exclaimed. "Thanks for letting us know, Pierre. I'll tell the others right away. Please give our best wishes to Jacques, and tell him we'll see him soon!"

She hung up and smiled at us. "Well?" George demanded impatiently.

"Is he all right?" René added.

"He's going to be fine," Bess reported. "Pierre told me that the doctor said Jacques was very lucky. He's shaken up and bruised, but there's no serious damage. He'll probably be released in a couple of hours."

"Oh, that is wonderful!" Thèo exclaimed.

"Yes," Bess agreed with a smile. "I think Pierre was relieved too. He was practically shouting into the phone."

I nodded. From what I knew of him so far, Pierre seemed quite impulsive and rather histrionic about life in general. In fact, while waiting for the ambulance after the fall, he had seemed more upset than Jacques himself about the accident.

René started pouring from the lemonade pitcher into the glasses Thèo had set on a little wicker table. "I think this calls for a toast," he exclaimed, handing the first glass to Bess with a little bow.

"Sounds good to . . ." My voice trailed off as I spotted someone striding down the sidewalk toward Simone's house. "Uh-oh," I finished in a small voice.

The others followed my gaze. "Who is that?" Thèo asked. "She seems to be coming this way."

I gulped. "It's my housekeeper, Hannah Gruen," I said. Just then Hannah spotted me and her frown deepened. "And I don't think she's coming for lemonade."

I spent the next hour in bed, after being soundly scolded by Hannah for wandering off when I was supposed to be resting. It turned out she had run into Mrs. Zucker at the store, and the woman mentioned what had just happened at Simone's house. Hannah had rushed home immediately to find me.

Although I couldn't blame her for being worried about me, I was disappointed not to have the chance to talk more with René and Thèo. I still felt as though the two guys were a mystery to me. Did one of them have a motive to want to steal the egg? I had no idea.

Luckily Bess and George had promised to step in again. We'd managed a brief, whispered conference before Hannah had dragged me off. My friends had planned to stay at Simone's and find out whatever they could about the two French guys, then come over and tell me what they'd learned.

Just because I couldn't be there helping them, though, it didn't mean I had to stop thinking about the case. I couldn't. I lay in my bed, staring thoughtfully at the ceiling as I turned over all the facts and speculations in my mind. I reviewed everything I knew about the people involved, the details of the crime. Once again I pondered motives. What would make one of Simone's friends steal a valuable, beloved heirloom from her?

For a moment I thought of Jacques again—he was the one who was so poor he couldn't afford the plane ticket here on his own. Maybe I was wrong about him. After all, I really didn't know him well.

Would the temptation of the egg just sitting there be enough of a motive? I wondered uneasily. It was a prime opportunity. . . .

I suddenly sat up in bed, finally realizing that there was one additional thing I hadn't been considering. As I heard a knock at my door the answer finally clicked into place in my head. Got it.

"Hi," Bess said as she and George entered. "You look happy. Does that mean your head is feeling better?"

"A little," I said, smiling. "What did you guys find out?"

George flopped onto the end of my bed. "Not a whole lot," she said. "But we did confirm that Jacques can't afford bus fare, let alone a new sports car. Thèo's jaw practically dropped off his face when I mentioned what Jacques had told you."

"However," Bess added smugly, "he also said that when Jacques likes a girl, he tends to make up wild stories to impress her. So I guess my theory was right!"

George shot her a glance. "Uh-huh," she said. "And speaking of crazy crushes, it would have been helpful if René hadn't been staring at you like a lovesick puppy the whole time we were trying to get information out of him." She turned to me with a shrug. "We couldn't get him to make any sense at all."

"Never mind," I told her. "I've been thinking about the case all afternoon. And I know who stole that Fabergé egg."

12

A Taste of Friendship

Bess and George just stared at me for a moment.

"Huh?" George said at last.

I smiled at their stunned expressions. "It was really kind of simple once I realized that we'd been spending all this time worrying about motive, when there was something else we should have been thinking about," I told them. "Opportunity."

"What do you mean?" Bess looked confused. "Didn't they all have the same opportunity? I mean, they were all in the house before it happened, right?"

"Right," I said. "Come on. I'll explain it on the way to Simone's. I want to go over there and confirm a couple of things."

Bess looked dubious. "Do you think Hannah will let you go?"

I shrugged. "Only one way to find out."

Miraculously, we were able to convince Hannah. She knows me well enough to realize that when I'm on the trail of a mystery, I can't think of anything else until it's solved. When I explained to her why I wanted to go to Simone's, she just sighed and waved me on my way.

"Just try not to hit your head on anything while you're en route, okay?" she called after me as I headed out the front door with my friends.

"Promise!" I called back over my shoulder.

Thèo and René seemed a little surprised to see us again so soon. Simone had returned from her shopping, and the guys had filled her in on what had happened to Jacques. Pierre and Jacques were still at the hospital, though they had called to say that Jacques was being released and they would be home soon.

After exchanging the latest news about Jacques's condition, which was still good, I asked Simone and the other two guys to sit down with us in the living room. "I think I've figured out what happened to your Fabergé egg," I told Simone.

She gasped, her eyes lighting up. "Really?" she cried. "What, Nancy? Please tell me, where is it?"

"I'll tell you in a second," I promised. "First, I need to ask you guys a couple of questions."

I started by explaining how my friends and I had

suspected Jacques for a while. "But I knew Jacques couldn't have done it, at least according to what the guys told us about the day it happened," I said. "Because as far as we know, he was never *alone* in the house before the egg disappeared." I turned to René and Thèo. "You guys said you arrived and almost immediately went out again. The only thing you did first was take your bags upstairs. And the three of you did that together, right?"

Thèo nodded. "Yes," he said, looking a little confused.

"And did Pierre come upstairs with you?" I continued.

"No," René put in. "Pierre pointed us toward the stairs, and the three of us went up and found our way to the guest room while he stayed behind to leave a note for Simone saying that we were going out for a while."

I nodded, not surprised. "That means the only one who was alone downstairs between the time Simone went out and the time you returned and found the egg missing was—"

"Pierre!" Simone finished for me with a gasp, her face going white.

"But we were only upstairs for a moment," René exclaimed. "Just long enough to set our bags in the guest room and use the bathroom upstairs."

I shrugged. "It wouldn't take long," I pointed out. "I'm sure Pierre knew exactly where the key to the glass case was—Simone didn't exactly have it hidden away. All he'd have to do is unlock the case, grab the egg and tuck it away somewhere to retrieve later, and wipe away his fingerprints."

Simone stood up, her face pinched and grim. "Are you saying that Pierre took the egg?" she exclaimed. "But why?"

I hesitated. "Well, I'm not totally sure," I said. "But I have a theory about that."

Simone didn't wait to hear it. She hurried out of the room, and we could hear her rapid footsteps on the stairs, then in the upstairs hallway. A moment later she returned.

George gasped, pointing to the object Simone held in her hands. "The egg!" she cried.

"I found it in Pierre's bag." Simone held up the heirloom with trembling hands. "I still can't believe—"

Just then we heard the front door open. A moment later Jacques walked in. He had a few bandages on his arms and legs and a large scrape on his forehead. But otherwise, he looked perfectly healthy.

"Hello, everyone," he said. "Pierre's parking the car. The hospital said I would probably survive, so they sent me . . ." His voice trailed off with a gulp as he suddenly noticed the Fabergé egg in Simone's hands. "Uh-oh," he said. "Where did you find it?"

"I think you know," I told him with a sympathetic smile. "You knew Pierre took it, didn't you?"

Jacques looked a little ill. "How did you find out?" he said, taking a step toward me. "I was pretty sure he had done it; I know him well enough to see that he wasn't acting quite himself. But I couldn't find the proof. I never had the opportunity to check his room—he was always right next to me." He shrugged. "After that first evening I wasn't even sure he still had it. But I checked in all of the local antique shops and didn't see any sign of it."

"Aha!" George exclaimed. "So that's why you went into those antique stores and stuff the day we were following you."

Bess elbowed her. "You mean the day we *ran into* him while we were out shopping."

The shadow of a smile flitted across Jacques's somber features. "It is okay," he told my friends. "I knew you were following me. I had only hoped it was because of the reason *Mademoiselle* Bess told me—that you lovely American ladies were madly in love with me."

Bess looked embarrassed. "Sorry," she said. "We were trying to help Nancy."

This time Jacques actually chuckled. Then his

expression went serious again as he glanced at Simone. "In any case," he said, "I soon realized that such an object was far too valuable to sell in a small city like River Heights. So I deduced that if Pierre had taken it, it must still be in the house. That's why I volunteered to go up the ladder today. I thought that would finally give me the chance to look in his room."

"I think Pierre must have realized that once you were up there," I said. I hesitated, not sure how to say the next part: that I was pretty sure Jacques's fall hadn't been an accident. Pierre must have yanked the ladder to cause the fall.

One look at Simone's face told me she had already figured it out, so I didn't bother to say it. I felt terrible for her. She had her heirloom back, but it had to be awful for her to know that her own nephew had been the culprit.

I opened my mouth, wanting to say something to make her feel better. But at that moment, Pierre walked into the room. When he saw us gathered there, he looked perplexed.

Then he saw the egg, and his face went white.

"Yum," I said, looking down at the grill. "Are there any more of those grilled zucchini slices?"

"Coming right up," Simone said with a smile,

reaching for the platter of sliced vegetables on a picnic table nearby.

"Thanks." I glanced around the tidy backyard. After Pierre had left a few days earlier, Simone had hired a local garden company to come in, clear away the weeds, and get her yard into shape. Now it looked great. The vegetable patch was bursting with produce, a formerly hidden rose garden had come back to life, and the level part of the lawn held not only the grill and picnic table, but several lounge chairs and wooden benches as well. At the moment, most of the lawn furniture was filled with Simone's new neighbors and friends. I could see Ned and Hannah sitting with some neighbors, plates balanced on their laps. Back by the wall overlooking the river, my father was chatting with Mrs. Zucker while little Owen played with a soccer ball nearby. And Mr. Geffington and Mr. Safer were standing together near the twining zucchini vines of the garden.

George and Bess wandered over toward the grill. "Great barbecue, Simone," George said. "If you keep having parties like this, with such great food, you're going to be the most popular person in the neighborhood!"

"Thanks, George." Simone smiled. "Of course, this party is mostly to thank you, Bess, and Nancy for helping me with my little problem last week." She glanced at me. "I'm so grateful for everything you did to help me get the egg back. And for supporting me afterward."

"I was happy to help," I said. I knew Simone still felt terrible about Pierre. Once he'd confessed to stealing the egg, Simone had called his family in France. Within two hours Pierre was on a plane on his way back home—to a very angry father. Simone had decided not to press charges, though she had assured us that her older brother, Pierre's father, would certainly punish his son when he got home.

"I still can't believe Pierre thought the egg was a fake," George commented, helping herself to a slice of grilled mushroom.

Bess nodded. "Now that you mention it, I'm still not sure I understand that part," she admitted. "Why did he want to steal a *fake* Fabergé egg?"

Simone sighed, shuffling the meat and vegetable slices that were grilling. "I think I've finally worked that out myself," she said. "You see, Pierre's father, André, is my older brother—much older, of course. I am the baby of the family, and my papa always doted on me a bit too much, I'm afraid. It often made my brother angry—not that he needed much of an excuse. He has quite a temper, just like Papa himself."

I nodded, picking up the explanation. "Simone mentioned something to me on the phone once about her father and Pierre's father not getting along. I'd meant to ask her about that, but I forgot about it for a while."

George feigned surprise. "Nancy Drew, forgetting to follow up on a clue?" she exclaimed teasingly.

I stuck my tongue out at her, then continued. "Anyway, I'd noticed all along that Pierre is pretty impulsive and hotheaded himself. Remember how he snapped at me at the party when he thought I was accusing his friends?"

George nodded and licked her fingers. "I figured that was just a guilty conscience or something."

"Maybe it was, partially," I said. "But it also showed that he doesn't always think things through before reacting. That's what happened with the egg, too. He heard that Simone was having the egg appraised that Monday, and took the first chance he got to snatch it."

"I get it," Bess said. "That ties in with what Simone told us after Pierre confessed, right?"

"That's right," I said. Simone had explained that her brother had always expected their father would leave him certain family valuables, including the egg.

Simone sighed. "It all seems so foolish, really," she said. "Papa died about ten years ago, having already given the egg to me, his baby. My mother knew that André wanted it, even though he was too proud to admit it. She had the fake made for him so that both of us could enjoy having the egg." She smiled sadly. "I think poor André felt terrible about fighting so much with Papa when he was alive. Once Papa died, he never made a peep to me about wanting the real egg back. Instead he treasured the fake as a reminder of Papa— and he never told anyone else that it wasn't real."

"How sad!" Bess said. "But do you mean all his life, Pierre thought his father had the real egg?"

Simone nodded, poking at a sizzling slice of onion. "In fact, André told little Pierre that he'd stolen the egg back from me, substituting a replica he'd had made. I don't know why he would make up such a tale— pride, I suppose. And that same pride made Pierre take the egg. He thought he was saving his father's good name by preventing the appraisal, since he feared I might figure out what had happened if the appraiser told me the egg was fake. He was willing to frame his good friends, even put Jacques in the hospital, to protect his father's reputation." She shrugged. "I guess he didn't realize I'd already had it appraised once, back in Paris. Or maybe he thought that appraisal happened before his father supposedly made the switch. I don't know. I suppose someday I'll ask him."

I nodded thoughtfully. I'd often noted that people's motives for committing crimes or doing other bad things were usually very simple—they wanted money, or revenge, or freedom, or some other basic thing. But in this case, I'd learned that motives could also be more complicated. There was no way I could have worked out that Pierre was the culprit by studying only motives in this case—not without a whole lot more information than I'd had at the time. Luckily I'd been able to figure it out by considering opportunity along with just a hint of possible motive.

"So did you have the appraisal done?" George asked Simone curiously.

Simone smiled. "Yes," she said. "And my egg is definitely the real one. Oh, and I've also bought a more theft-proof display box for it . . . just in case!"

Bess leaned on the picnic table. "That's good," she said. "I guess Jacques must have been pretty angry with Pierre about all this, huh? I mean, first he tries to frame him, then he knocks him off that ladder."

"Yes, of course." Simone looked sad. "It's a shame. They have been friends for many years. I hope they work things out."

At that moment I saw Mr. Geffington and Mr. Safer walking toward the grill holding empty paper plates. I smiled at the sight of them chatting away with each other.

At least one friendship—against all odds—seems to have survived the past week, I thought.

"Better put some more zucchini on the grill," I

told Simone as the men approached. "Mr. Geffington is probably going to eat up all you have, since his garden won't have any until his new set of plants set fruit."

Bess giggled. "At least this time he won't have to worry about them getting smashed, now that you finally ferreted out the culprit, Nancy."

"That reminds me," Simone said. "Could you watch the grill for a moment? I have something cooking inside that should be just about ready."

We nodded. For the next few minutes, we were busy serving Mr. Geffington, Mr. Safer, and several others from the grill.

As I was flipping over some slices of eggplant, Chief McGinnis approached.

"Well, well, Miss Drew," he greeted me with a not-quite-happy smile. "I was just talking to your father. He tells me you are the one responsible for solving our little zucchini problem."

I knew why the chief of police didn't sound particularly pleased with me. Not only had I cracked the case of the missing egg before his officers had even come up with any leads, but I'd also solved the zucchini case right under his nose. He probably didn't mind that—like my father, he probably thought it was much ado about nothing—except that Mr. Geffington had given a long, glowing quote about me to the local newspaper without mentioning the police department at all.

I decided it was a good time to make nice. After all, there was no telling when I might need the chief's help for another case, so I always tried to stay on his good side. "Yes, I suppose I did figure that one out," I admitted pleasantly. "But it was really sort of an accident."

"Literally," George put in helpfully. "She figured it out by falling on her head."

The chief looked slightly confused. "I see," he said, even though he clearly didn't.

Bess took pity on him. "Nancy slipped on Mr. Geffington's front steps on Saturday night," she explained. "At the time, we thought that the egg thief might have pushed her or something, since she's usually not that clumsy. But a couple of days later Mr. Geffington mentioned that the zucchini smasher had struck again on Saturday night, and that he'd had to clean sticky, slimy zucchini goo off his front steps."

"So we realized that Nancy must've slipped on the goo," George finished.

The chief still looked perplexed. "Yes, yes," he said. "But, er . . ."

I could tell he still didn't understand how I'd figured out who had destroyed the zucchini. "After that, I put two and two together," I told him. "See,

146

when Simone's friend Jacques fell off the ladder, the house was locked. So I had to run across the street to call for help. I knew that Mrs. Zucker works at home, so I went straight there. Little Owen was in the driveway with his baseball bat, which he handed to me when he ran in to get his mother. I barely noticed at the time, but later on I remembered that the handle was sticky and slimy—just like Mr. Geffington described his steps."

George clearly noticed that the chief still didn't look enlightened. "So that's when she realized that Owen's baseball bat was the, er, murder weapon. So to speak."

I was still proud of myself for that bit of deduction, though I wished I'd have figured it out earlier. Still, with all the commotion over the missing egg, it was no wonder that the zucchini issue had taken a backseat for a while. In any case, as soon as I'd thought a little harder about that sticky bat, it all started to make sense. At Mrs. Mahoney's house that day, Mrs. Zucker had mentioned that little Owen hated zucchini. When Ned and I were at Susie Lin's restaurant, she had also mentioned that Owen and his friends had come in and made comments about the zucchini fritters on her menu. And of course, everyone knew that all week Mrs. Zucker had been going house to house through the neighborhood, collecting money for the Anvil Day celebration. While she was inside chatting with the neighbors, Owen had been outside demolishing all examples of his least favorite vegetable with his toy bat. Mr. Safer had even mentioned seeing the pair on the night that Mr. Geffington's garden had been struck.

I'd mentioned my suspicions first to Mrs. Zucker, who had spied on her young son just long enough to catch him in the act and confirm my theory. Then she had apologized to Mr. Geffington and the other neighbors who had been affected. Mr. Geffington apologized to Mr. Safer. Little Owen had been justly punished by the removal of all TV and dessert privileges for the next month. And luckily Simone's zucchini patch was growing vigorously enough that it would probably supply the whole neighborhood.

"Well, all's well that ends well," I said lightly, glancing over at Owen. He was trailing behind his mother as she wandered over to the beverage table. I'd noticed that he was sticking close to her, and guessed that he was under strict orders not to get out of her sight.

Bess giggled. "It's really kind of funny now that we know what happened."

"Hmm. Yes, I suppose." Chief McGinnis didn't seem very amused. "Well, I hope that boy has learned his lesson."

"I'm sure he has," I said politely, hiding my own smile until the chief had wandered away.

A few minutes later my friends and I were chatting with Mrs. Zucker when Simone emerged from the house. She was carrying a large platter piled high with greenish beige pancakes.

"Are those——," Bess began as Simone set down the platter on the picnic table.

"Yep," Simone interrupted with a wink before she could finish the question. "Susie Lin gave me the recipe herself." She cleared her throat. "Want one, Owen?" she asked. "I think you'll really like them."

Mrs. Zucker glanced at the platter and chuckled. But she kept quiet as Simone put one of the zucchini fritters on a plate.

"Here you go," she said. "Try it, you'll like it!"

Owen accepted the plate and stared at the fritter suspiciously. "What is it?" he asked.

"Potato pancakes," George spoke up. "Right, guys?"

Simone nodded and smiled, and the rest of us quickly agreed. Owen glanced up at his mother.

"Go ahead, take a taste," she urged him. "You like potatoes, remember?"

Owen carefully lifted the fritter to his mouth. He bit off a tiny piece and chewed carefully. Then he took a larger bite.

"Mmm," he mumbled through the half-chewed

fritter. "I like potatoes! Can I have another one, please?"

I was pretty sure that Owen had no idea why all the grown-ups suddenly started laughing. But as he gobbled down several more zucchini fritters, I guessed that he probably didn't care.

She's sharp.

She's smart.

She's confident.

She's unstoppable.

And she's on your trail.

MEET THE NEW NANCY DREW

Still sleuthing,

still solving crimes,

but she's got some new tricks up her sleeve!

NANCY DREW

girl detective

star power

by Catherine Hapka

She's beautiful, she's talented, she's famous.

She's a star!

Things would be perfect if only her family was around to help her celebrate. . . .

Follow the adventures of fourteen-year-old pop star **Star Calloway**

A new series from Simon & Schuster